THE DEAD FALL

DI OLIVIA AUSTIN - BOOK TWO

NIC ROBERTS

Copyright © 2021 by Nic Roberts

The Dead Fall'

All rights reserved.
No part of this book may be reproduced in any form or by any electronic or mechanical means, including information storage and retrieval systems, without written permission from the author, except for the use of brief quotations in a book review.
This is a work of fiction. Names characters, places and incidents either are the product of the author's imagination or are used fictitiously. Some may be used for parody purposes.

Any resemblance to events, locales, business establishments, or actual persons living or dead is purely coincidental.

LOVE TO READ DETECTIVE THRILLERS?

Join my Newsletter to be the first to hear about New Releases and ARC opportunities.

http://eepurl.com/hskzML

THE DEAD FALL

What's done in the dark will always come to light... A hideous crime with many layers. This one will either make or break her.

After the dramatic conclusion of last month's missing girl case, Detective Inspector Olivia Austin feels as though she's finally finding her feet.

With a strong budding friendship in DI Dean Lawrence and a team that finally believes she's fit for the job, life with Newquay CID could only get better, but the discovery of a deceased male on the ground beneath his balcony shakes a sleepy coastal community.

With injuries not quite adding up, Olivia must work hard to unravel the mystery that surrounds his death. With dark secrets rising to the surface, she needs to find out, do the dead fall, or was he pushed?

PROLOGUE

He was better off dead.
No, it was worse than that. In reality, he'd been dead for many years already, forcing his way through the bleak routines of his life. Wake up. Eat. Work. Sleep. Repeat. Until he'd met *her*.

Each day was the same variant of that repetitive misery and now, as he stood on the bleak ledge of the balcony at his rented one-bedroom apartment, he knew it had to stop.

It wasn't particularly high, but it was nonetheless high enough to make sure that when he fell, he'd never have to feel this way ever again.

His phone back in the lounge sounded. A guardian angel perhaps? Maybe it was her. He *hoped* it was her, but she wouldn't care enough; and he knew that. Especially after what he'd done, the hurt and pain he'd caused her.

As he reflected on his pitiful existence at the edge of his miserably small balcony, he knew he deserved it. Still, that didn't mean she had to sever everything they'd worked so hard for over the past twelve years.

God, he loved her. He closed his eyes and imagined her premature greying brown hair, knotted and messy when she woke up from a night of intense sex, or the single dimple that appeared whenever she was deep in thought. Her grey eyes always reminded him of the ocean on a bleak, cloudy day. There was so much power and *life* in them. Forever churning, forever moving. She was the best thing that had ever happened to him. What the hell had he been thinking?

He'd convinced himself that he never wanted to see those things again and that jumping would be the only answer, but now, as he stood on top of what felt like the edge of the world with the wind gently caressing his face, he started to have doubts.

Despite everything that he'd done, he knew this would destroy her. He knew it would eat away at her soul for the rest of her life, and he didn't know if that was what he wanted anymore.

It took only that one simple thought, a simple drop in the ocean of chaos he faced, to turn the tide for him. He climbed down. *I can show her. I can be better for her.*

He turned back toward the lounge just as his front door opened.

Oh? I thought I'd locked that.

"Lydia?" he heard himself call out, smoothing his

hands down against his trousers, wiping away the last remnants of his fear, emboldened with each passing step. "I'm glad you..."

He stopped as he entered the hall and came face to face with his new company.

"Wait..." he growled, holding his hand out to keep the distance between them. "I said I was..." He turned back toward the lounge, ready to run, but caught his foot on the rug—the one he'd been adamant he didn't want to buy—and landed in a crumpled heap partially beneath the coffee table.

He tried to pull himself back up, but a boot clad foot came down hard on his back.

"Stay down, Arsehole!" the voice hissed, and he felt the pressure crunching a vertebra in his back. "After I've finished with you, you're going to wish you had jumped."

1

"For fuck's sake, we need back up!" Olivia screamed into her radio. "Code red! Officer down!"

The words almost stuck in her throat, and she barely managed to muster enough strength to say them. Her years of training had prepared her for a scenario like this, but now, as it was happening, it felt surreal. It was as though she wasn't standing there experiencing it for herself.

She knelt down beside her partner DCI Rhys Thomas as he pressed his fingers against the neck of their uniformed colleague, whose body was splayed out on the floor in front of them, trying to stem the spurting blood.

"Fuck we need that back up, like yesterday!" he growled. "They've left us here like sitting ducks!"

Olivia swallowed back the unmistakable churn of panic in her stomach.

"It has to be us," she hissed. "We can't wait! The public need us, you're right. They need someone on scene!"

She heard what sounded like bullets ricocheting off the walls. How the hell had guns managed to make their way over here? Without being armed herself, what chance did she have against them?

His eyes met hers, and immediately he knew what she was thinking.

"No!" Rhys said firmly. "You have to stay until they get here. They're on their way."

She pulled herself to standing, unable to block out the high-pitched screams she could hear. The sounds of death and panic swarmed her, drowning her in the despair of it all. She moved as if weighed down by invisible weights; everything felt ridiculously more difficult than it should have.

"I'm going," she answered defiantly. "I have to. I can't sit here and do nothing. Stay with Jacobson..."

Rhys grabbed hold of her arm tightly before she could run off.

"*You* stay here!" he ordered. "Keep pressure on his neck until the ambulance arrives and I'll go. I'm not losing you today!"

What sounded like a small IED rocked the already broken air and Olivia jumped around. There was no time to discuss who got to do what. Rhys was the trained medic out of the two of them. Their colleague needed him. He knew that, too.

"When the ambulance gets here," she started, hearing the panic and fear in her own voice, "find me. I'm going along Poland Street!"

The wail of sirens and blue lights erupted around them as the police backup landed on scene. Olivia ran alongside the officers to brief them; she was quick and to the point.

Just as she went to disappear around the corner, she cast one more look over her shoulder at her partner. Their eyes met. Calm against the chaos. The deep breath the air takes in the eye of a storm. His gentle soul radiating to her from where he knelt. She felt peace.

DETECTIVE INSPECTOR OLIVIA AUSTIN woke up drenched in sweat again despite the cool temperature of her surroundings. Everything slowly faded into focus from her nightmare-induced panic as she brought herself down from the terror with deep breaths. The room was unfamiliar to her—dark mahogany walls, framed abstract art and a photo of a smiling young man and his dog on the bedside table.

A body stirred beside her and she held her breath... *no!* Then, it all came back to her. Susan's birthday party. Just a couple of drinks they'd said. Her pounding head suggested she clearly hadn't stopped after two.

The body stirred again, and a lean muscular leg

stretched out from the side of the navy duvet. Then a head lifted up.

Olivia groaned inwardly, wincing as lucidity came back to her.

They belonged to a certain Police Constable Andrew Shaw, or Duracell, as she'd heard a couple of the other women call him. Supposedly he had an impeccable amount of energy.

He looked at her before a slow easy smile spread across his handsome features and he ran a hand through his messy dark hair. Chocolate eyes met her squinting green ones.

"Shit, Shaw!" she hissed, still feeling a tad groggy. "Did we?" She rubbed sleep from her eyes. *At least he's a good-looking one*, she thought to herself.

His grin widened and he shook his head.

"No…unfortunately not," he replied with the shake of his head. A classic Olivia quirked eyebrow prompted him to speak more. "You passed out and it was the gentlemanly thing to do, you know, putting you to bed here. I didn't have your address when we were in the taxi…"

Olivia climbed out from beneath the covers, her crumpled black dress ridden up to expose more of her thighs than she thought any co-worker at Newquay had seen. Still, her hips and waist had stayed covered, and she was quick to shimmy the body-tight dress further down her legs whilst blowing stray hairs out of her face.

She let out a loud groan. *What are you, fresh out of uni?* She scolded herself.

At least Shaw was doing his best to avert his gaze.

"I would have taken up on the couch for the evening," he told her. "But you said you wanted me to stay with you. Besides, what kind of man would I be to leave you alone that drunk? You could have choked on your own vomit!"

Olivia rolled her eyes before turning back to face him.

"Thank you, but *this* didn't happen," she warned Shaw, pointing at him as if to emphasise how serious she was. The pounding in her head made it hard to feel serious about anything, however.

"My lips are sealed," he promised, gesturing across his mouth. "Hey, not to pry or anything, but you didn't seem to sleep too well. You seemed a bit...*disturbed?*"

Olivia blinked back the embarrassment.

"Try being on the force for twelve years then let me know how well you sleep afterwards," she shot back, hiding behind a vague reference to the badge rather than face the real reason that she lived in a constant state of nightmares. The sweat from her dreams of Rhys still clung to the nape of her neck.

"Touché," Shaw replied with a lazy smile. "Well listen, I feel bad that I wasn't able to get you home last night. I can at least cook you breakfast to make up for it if you'd like?"

Olivia blanched, a bit shocked at the offer.

"Um—"

The sound of a phone ringing cut though her words; it took her a moment to realise that it wasn't hers.

Andrew leaned over, revealing more of his taut muscles as he reached for the phone on his bedside table.

"Nurofen's on your side." He gestured before accepting the call.

Olivia quickly palmed two and dry swallowed before walking away from the admittedly extremely comfortable bed of PC Shaw.

She took a moment to slide the curtain open a little and peek through at the calm morning, immediately regretting it after she felt a sharp pain in her head. Luckily, Nurofen was a quick remedy for any hangover she'd ever dealt with. The sooner she located her shoes and bag, the sooner she could get back home and hope to put this whole episode behind her. She didn't want to make getting involved with colleagues a recurring thing. Especially being so new to this station, she'd prefer not to create waves with drama.

And the last time she'd seriously done that, she'd ended up standing next to his mother while she broke into pieces at his funeral.

The nightmare. Her own personal hell, repeating time and time again. It was always that moment—the time she last saw Rhys. She wished she could see different versions of the event, like what would have happened if she'd done as he told her, if she'd been the one to stay back with Jacobson. Where would she be now? She let herself remember that long-gone paradise: their modest flat on the edge of London with the nosey neighbours, the plant that had mysteriously turned up at their front door, the unrepentant smoke alarm, and the burn stain from *that* candle incident. It brought a fresh wave of tears to her eyes. She tried not to dwell on that place. It stood as one more reminder of all that she'd lost that day.

After that initial pang, though, her chest warmed, and a smile crossed her lips. As much as it hurt, it was still a good memory. *That's new.*

"Sorry, Olivia?"

She pulled herself back to reality and glared at Andrew as he held the phone out to her.

She waved him away silently with her hand.

"Collins," he elaborated with a pointed look. "He already knew you were here."

Olivia rolled her eyes, took the deepest breath she could muster, and placed the phone by her ear.

"Sir, whatever you think happened, it really di—"

"DI Austin," he chided, not waiting nor caring for her response. She turned away from Andrew's smug grin. He was enjoying this far too much.

"Sorry, yes? Is everything okay?" she asked.

She heard his weary sigh from the other end of the phone. He was a hardworking man, and she could always put her money on the fact that he'd be the first one in the office every morning. Rumour had it that he'd once spent a week's annual leave in the staff room *'just in case'* he was needed. She had a lot of time for him, but it was only since last night that she'd learned a few of the other detectives referred to him as 'Grumps' and she couldn't un-hear it.

"Apologies for interrupting," he continued, his tone grave. "I wouldn't normally spring on you like this, you know that. Especially after..."

"...Susan's party," Olivia finished quickly before he said anything else.

There was a pause.

"Yes, indeed. Well," he cleared his throat. "There's been a murder, and I'd like your team on the case."

Olivia turned on her professional mode and left the confines of Andrew's masculine bedroom and went out into the hall.

"Male or female?" she asked, making her way to where she assumed the lounge was. "And can I ask why you didn't try *my* mobile?"

Another pause.

"We have," he answered. "Both myself and DI Lawrence did."

A half-dressed male torso emerged from behind one of the other doors and Olivia paused, trying to keep her eyes trained on his and nowhere below. She shot him her dirtiest look.

He held his hands up, amused.

"Sorry!" he whispered.

She mouthed it back and pressed forward on the

hunt for her bag. She barely even remembered the building, let alone talking to PC Shaw enough to end up in his bed. Her cheeks flushed as she thought back to the hazy night.

"Are you there, Olivia?" Collins asked.

"Sorry, yes I am, I'm just a little..." She found a half-scrunched up shopping list on the side and a pen on the floor. She wedged the phone between her shoulder and ear and lowered herself to the sofa. "Right, did you say female?"

The bloody pen didn't work. She licked the tip of the biro.

"Male," he corrected. "Late 30s. Found on the ground beneath the balcony of his flat."

Odd.

"Murder did you say?" she asked. "How are we sure it wasn't suicide?"

Collins mused something to someone out of earshot before returning to her. He had a knack for multiple conversations at once.

"Forensics will be onsite shortly," he said back to her. "And the first officers on scene reckon he might have been dead *or* dying before he fell. He's got bruising around his neck consistent with strangulation, injuries inconsistent with *only* a fall... I need you there Olivia. Your team is one of our best. Lawrence is already on route to pick you up."

She looked down at her scalloped lace top black dress.

"Oh, but I'm not—"

The line went dead.

"Hung up on you?"

Olivia jumped round to see PC Shaw rested against the door frame, her bag dangling from his finger.

"Were you looking for this?" he asked.

Olivia stood up and snatched it from him.

"Just because I made an error in judgement doesn't mean I'm destined to repeat it," she warned. "Especially a *drunken* one."

He followed her through the hall and stopped behind her when she located the bathroom.

"Is that a challenge, boss?" he asked with a sly smile.

Olivia rinsed her mouth under the tap before Andrew handed her an unopened toothbrush.

She glared back at him in disgust.

"I see you fully earned your name."

She took it from him as he laughed.

"Relax." The amusement across his face was monumental. "I happened to have bought a few spares for when I travel. Nothing seedy."

He watched her as she brushed her teeth and then followed her further down the hall to the door where she maneuvered into her court shoes.

"Can I drive you anywhere?" he asked. "Just give me a second to get dressed. I'm not one for letting women wander out into taxis..."

She stopped and turned to him, giving him the full attention that he deserved.

He was much younger than she was. That was the main problem. Still at the start of his policing career. The part where every film and tv documentary series made police work look fun and thrilling and he'd joined for that ride. His eyes were blazing with the innocent cheekiness that only came about with his age, and she could easily see why she'd had a catastrophic lapse in rational thinking and followed him into the taxi. He'd also been her saviour when Samuel Mercer from the Hebden case had tossed her to the side like a rag doll the previous month. Seeing him turn up had given her renewed vigour. Perhaps that had something to do with the soft spot she seemed to have for him.

He was charming. She had to give him that.

"Detective Lawrence is coming to get me," she answered and watched the frown spread across his chiselled features.

"If he must." He sighed, frowning at her words. "Can I at least make you a coffee and that breakfast I promised? A Bacon Butty for the road? Give you some clothes to change into?"

Olivia looked back down at her black dress. It did look slightly overdressed to turn up and survey a crime scene with, but anything had to be better than arriving at the scene dressed in Shaw's clothes. Fuck, the thought made her cringe inwardly. She could suffice in swaddling herself in her coat.

"Honestly, I'm fine. Thank you," she added reluctantly. "Thank you for being respectful." That statement she actually meant.

He reached up and pulled her coat down from the hook for her.

"I would say call me, but..."

She gave him a warning glare that morphed into a smile when she saw his cheeky grin.

"Now go and put yourself some clothes on, for goodness' sake!" she scolded before she closed the front door and put that most mystifying event behind her.

2

"Don't say anything." The words were out of Olivia's lips before she had even entered the car. Detective Inspector Dean Lawrence gave her a small look before easing the car back into drive. Olivia bit the corner of her bottom lip, struggling to peel her eyes away from the road and towards her partner.

"Nothing happened," she muttered, brushing her hair out of her face once again. She wished she had a hairband of some sort to put it all away.

"It's none of my business," Lawrence replied. He offered her the end of a phone charging cable and gratefully she plugged her mobile in. "But Duracell? I'm dying to know if he lives up to his name?"

That earned him a gentle smack, but Olivia couldn't help but realise that it felt good to see her partner's wry grin. He did a good job of breaking the ice.

"Again, it didn't happen," Olivia warned.

Lawrence looked over at her again. *I know*, his eyes whispered beneath their amused sparkle.

"Regardless, I mean it, it's completely none of my business," he said aloud. "I did, however, nose around under your desk and found your bag of spare clothes."

He nodded with his head to the back seat. Olivia's eyebrows shot up unbidden.

"You did *not*," she admonished, turning to see her rather unstylish *Sports Direct* duffel bag behind her seat. "Dean…thank you," she breathed.

"My pleasure," he replied, another smile dancing across his lips. "I also got a black coffee from the station for you too." He gestured to the cupholder on her side. "Tim's finest."

Olivia almost let out a squeal.

"I owe you one," she spoke excitedly.

Lawrence huffed before giving a gentle nod, his face back to all shades of seriousness.

"Listen," he said, his voice lowered a fraction. "Not to get all 'protective brother' on you, but I think you should be wary regarding Shaw."

Olivia turned to him, eyebrow quirked.

"I know how to handle myself, Dean," she chided, manoeuvring herself so she could reach into her bag to pull her clothes into the front seat. Her younger years as a ballet student had taught her how to change surprisingly well inside the confines of a moving vehicle. She started shimmying the trousers on.

"I know you do, Liv. Sorry, I shouldn't overstep," Lawrence mumbled before glancing over to Olivia. His eyes shot back to the road as soon as he realised she was changing in the car.

"Don't worry, Detective, I won't flash you," she teased. "And you're not overstepping, I suppose. But honestly, I can handle myself."

Lawrence sighed, brow creasing.

"I know you can," he admitted, hands notably flexing on the steering wheel. "I just don't want him to *use* you, Liv."

His concern for her welfare warmed her a little, and she gave him a reassuring smile.

"Trust me," she responded gently. "If one of us were to use the other, it wouldn't be Shaw using me. I *am* the superior officer, after all."

She had managed to pull her trousers over her hips and began slipping her arms out of the dress's straps, being careful to keep the top of it high enough to cover her chest.

"Just don't lose sleep over it, yeah?" Lawrence pressed, glancing over briefly at Olivia.

She hummed in agreement, pulling the sleeves of her blouse on. She started buttoning it, gently smiling to herself. *Still got it.*

"I'll try my best," she replied with as much confidence as she could muster. "So, did *you* end up leaving Susan's 50th with anyone? I think the last time I saw you, she was trying to set you up with her daughter!"

Lawrence laughed at the memory.

"Oh well, clearly, I stayed at Susan's and we had a torrid love affair that the Greek poets would have memorialised for centuries had they witnessed it," he deadpanned.

Olivia gave him another light smack.

"Unfortunately, my love life has been rather dry recently," he quietly admitted. "I promised myself I'd take a break."

"The legendary Dean Lawrence, taking a break from dating?" Olivia asked, her eyebrow raised as she finished buttoning her shirt. "How will all the local ladies cope?"

She was well aware of his reputation with women, despite his deep denial.

"I know, what a shock." He grinned, with an eye roll for effect. "What will all the tabloids have to say?" He glanced over to Olivia again. "That was bloody impressive, by the way."

"What, spending the night with Duracell and not actually sleeping with him?" Olivia asked with a scoff. "I'm not that susceptible to manly charms, believe it or not."

"I meant your quick change, Casanova," Lawrence shot back.

Olivia chuckled.

"Oh. Why, thank you," she murmured. An image of herself climbing into a taxi crept its way into her mind and she cringed. "So, changing the subject… How many people know I left the party with Shaw?"

Lawrence nodded slowly.

"You want the truth?" he asked.

"All of it," she answered, not knowing if she really wanted to hear it.

Beside her, Dean took a deep breath.

"Pretty much everyone and their mum's uncle's cousin's dog," he replied unable to hide his amusement. "I believe Trina was the one who shut the taxi door..."

"Well shit," Olivia sighed. "I'm going to have to insist you start dating again so that I'm not the staff room gossip subject for the rest of the year."

"I'll think about it," Lawrence teased. "You'd owe me one though." He turned down the radio a fraction more. "We're almost on scene now. I guess I should brief you before we get there. Our victim's name is Simon Fisher. He was a high school teacher a stone's throw from where he lived. Recently separated from his wife, Lydia Fisher. We got the call around 7 a.m. Neighbour left the building to start his shift and saw him—or rather, what's left of him." Olivia nodded with each fact. "We've got a couple of uniforms canvassing the building to see if anyone heard something in the night or early this morning. Just us on scene today. DC Harris won't be in, so we've been given a PC to help us."

Their car pulled up alongside the police cordon and Olivia checked her watch. There were already a number of people on site. The ambulance crew had started packing up their equipment, although the medical examiner stayed next to the body, covered in a white sheet. A tent was already pitched nearby with a couple of officers consulting with the forensics team.

She looked across at Lawrence as he turned off the engine. Before she had the opportunity to make a grim or witty remark, a knock came at his window. A young female officer, brown hair pulled messily into a bun, looked into the car, a hint of too much giddiness splayed across her face. Olivia perked an eyebrow.

"Remind me how long it's been since you've taken a break from dating?" she asked with a smirk.

Lawrence wordlessly passed her the coffee he had retrieved from the station before climbing out of the car, ending their conversation before she could press him further. Olivia took a sip of the now lukewarm liquid, set it back into the cup holder, and then straightened her clothes as she followed him out of the vehicle. Despite being able to quickly swap out of her evening clothes, she knew her face still held traces of last night's makeup. Plus, she hadn't gotten an opportunity to properly readjust her hair. Goodness, even the bright eyed and bushy tailed policewoman standing beside her partner had sussed that out. She could tell by the way she gave her a brief once over.

"Let's do this," Olivia declared, pushing confidence through her lungs and out of her lips. Lawrence nodded, stepping forward towards the grisly crime scene.

"Reece," The young officer smiled, turning to her.

Rhys? For a moment, Olivia's breath caught in the back of her throat. She gave a perfunctory glance across the scene at hand, surveying her surroundings before facing her colleague again. *How on earth did she know about him?*

"What...?" she started, but Lawrence rested a firm hand on her elbow.

"PC *Bethany* Reece," he said steadily and offered her a raised eyebrow to check she was okay.

She nodded, the crimson heat of her embarrassment overlooked by the Constable in front of her who smiled, oblivious to the comparisons drawn from her name.

"Oh, yes," Olivia breathed resting a hand on the woman's arm. "Pleased to meet you. DI Olivia Austin."

With introductions made, the trio made their way over to the crime scene.

Despite the pit in her stomach and the trip of her heartbeat into a quicker pulse, she knew it was all some foolish cruelty of mismatched wires after a lack of a good night's sleep.

It didn't quell the sinking feeling in her chest to know that, though.

3

"Catch us up," Lawrence ordered, walking with Olivia towards the crime scene. She did her best to shake the name mishap from her mind. *Focus on the case.* She let her eyes wander, observing a distraught woman near the entrance of the building. She appeared to be in her mid-30s. *Close to the victim?*

A man appeared at Lawrence's side with the scene log, which he signed seamlessly.

"The deceased is one Simon Fisher," PC Reece explained, walking with the detective pair towards the cordon. Her voice made her sound like an overeager puppy, and Olivia pursed her lips in an attempt to not show how greatly this interaction was amusing her. Just what she needed to lighten the mood. "I'm assuming you've gotten the details of the fall. I'll let Dr. James give you the full run down of his findings."

Shit, Olivia thought to herself. As they got closer, it became more and more apparent that they were approaching the charming new medical examiner that Olivia had been introduced to on the Hebden case. *And now I'm showing up like this, after everyone at the station thinks I've had a quickie with a fiendish constable.*

"...we've got the wife over there—Lydia Fisher," the policewoman continued. "She's in some sort of shock. She wants to talk with you both once you've examined the scene."

"Great, thank you so much for your briefing, Constable." Lawrence's voice was overly diplomatic, and Olivia could tell he was purposefully refraining from using her last name. The woman looked a bit crestfallen at his stoic attitude.

"Well. Let me know if you need anything else, Dean. It's good to see you." The last sentence was barely above a whisper. She let her gaze hit the cobblestone until the end of her statement, a hopeful smile dancing across her lips as her eyes lifted up to look at his. He gave her a gentle smile and quick nod before pacing off with Olivia.

"Want talk about it?" she asked her partner without turning to face him.

"Nah," he huffed. "I should be asking you that, though?"

She sighed and shook her head.

"The name just caught me off guard," she answered.

"That's all. Coupled with terrible sleep and a slight hangover."

Lawrence glanced down at her.

"Do you need a break?" He asked. "I can call one of the others to attend instead."

Olivia stopped him with a hand to his arm.

"Don't, Dean," she said firmly. "I'm okay. You know that. It was just an easy mix-up. I'm fine."

He nodded and gave her a smile.

"I know you are."

They continued their short walk and Lawrence paused at the tent to pull overshoes and gloves on. Olivia followed suit, the tell-tale snap of latex covering her hands so routine it barely registered to her as something she was doing. She did a cursory glance around the tent to see if she recognised any of the officers. She quickly realised that while the faces may have seemed vaguely familiar, there wasn't anyone she was close with already on scene.

Does that make it better or worse for the gossip mill? she idly wondered to herself as she led the way over to the body covered by the white sheet. Her heels—still left over from the night before—clicked resolutely against the cobblestone despite the overshoes covering them. *What a way to show up to a crime scene*, she mused internally.

She winced at the state of herself when Dr. James turned to face her. He stood tall against the grey sky, mostly hidden in his white over-suit. His dark brown eyes held such mystery and depth. His lips perked up into a smile upon seeing Olivia and Lawrence. She felt her lips mirror the doctor's motions. It was hard to resist whatever magnetism he had about him.

"Greetings, Detectives," he declared, ushering the pair closer to the body of Simon Fisher. "I'd like to show you some details on the body, if that's all right with you." There was such sincerity in his voice it nearly overwhelmed Olivia. She silently thanked the medical examiner for not commenting on her dramatic makeup or stiletto heels as they walked onto the stepping plates.

"Good morning, Dr. James," Lawrence offered up, gently breaking Olivia's reverie. "Let's see what you've got."

The medical examiner gave a curt nod, bending down to lift the sheet off of Simon's corpse.

Olivia steadied her breathing as the sheet revealed a pale white man in pyjama bottoms and a stained old blue robe. His haphazardly splayed corpse was strewn across the paving stones in a way that was subtly unnatural—bodies broke in such strange ways when they landed from a fall. She noted some bone fragments amongst the scattered flesh. Caked blood obscured a fair amount of his already downturned face, although he seemed to be a rather average looking man in his late-30s.

Olivia could feel bile rise in her throat. She struggled with victims who had fallen to their deaths; there was something about it that twisted a knot in her stomach.

She shuddered as she thought about the time between Mr. Fisher's departure into a free fall and his untimely marriage to the cement. How would those brief seconds have felt? Could you still hope for another chance, or did you have to make your peace quickly? Did the time stretch into what felt like eternity, or was it over before you had the opportunity to properly register what was happening to you?

"First, we've got some bruising around the victim's neck," Dr. James explained, gesturing in the air above the blemishes with a pen to draw attention to the area. Sure enough, subtle welts of purple marks circled Mr. Fisher's neck like a chain. "It's possible that some of the bruising could have been caused by the fall, but it seems doubtful that it would appear on his neck, and in such a clear pattern at that."

Olivia nodded.

"What else could indicate foul play?" she inquired, peering closer to see the bruising better. It definitely reminded her of some of the strangling victims she had seen in her London days, although it wasn't quite to that extreme.

"There are also some lacerations on his back even though he fell on his stomach," Dr. James elaborated. His gloved fingers gingerly picked up the bottom of the robe and pulled it up to display Simon Fisher's back. It didn't look pretty. Dozens of small cuts criss-crossed Simon's back, like a modern painting focusing on small red dashes.

"How do we know these weren't caused by the fall?" Lawrence chimed in.

"These wounds are quite close to the surface of the skin; in order to sustain that kind of injury, he'd have to interact with something raking across his back." Dr James explained. "Perhaps glass or the corner of a heavy object. Regardless, the pathway of his fall suggests he went over the balcony, not through any glass while on his way down. And from the angle he splatted, there's no way that hitting the ground would have generated injuries on his back."

He spoke with ease, readjusting Mr. Fisher's robe as he did. Looking to the detectives, he covered the man's body after they gave him a resolute nod, rising after the sheet fell over their victim.

"So, we're nearly positive that foul play was a part of this." Lawrence sighed with a nod. "Makes sense. Is there anything else we should know at this point, Doc?"

Dr. James smiled.

"You two are free to call me Elliot, you know," he replied with that same small twinkle in his eye. Olivia let herself really take in his features as he spoke. She hadn't ever seen him outside of the harsh fluorescents of his office. Even though it was a cloudy, windy day, his lightly tanned skin seemed to glow with life in the outdoors. His dark hair clearly was well-groomed and his eyes… Olivia kept coming back to those dark brown eyes.

"That's all I've got for you as of yet," Elliot replied.

"I'll be sure to give you a ring if there's anything that comes up on the autopsy."

"Thank you, Dr. James," Olivia replied with a warm smile, once more pulling a strand of her hair out of the clutches of the wind and away from her face.

"Elliot," he gently reminded her, warmth infused in his voice. "The pleasure is all mine, Detectives. We'll be in touch."

"Agreed," Olivia offered up with a smile. "Elliot." That got her a nod before Dr. James turned on his heel and walked towards his team to start directing the transport of Mr. Fisher's corpse.

"Let's talk with the wife then," Lawrence sighed, giving Simon Fisher's covered body one last look before glancing to Olivia.

"What makes someone want to beat a guy up and *then* shove him off a balcony?" she mused with the gentle shake of a head.

"Hopefully, we find out soon," Lawrence replied, beginning to lead the charge towards the entrance to the apartment building. He pulled up the cordon to let Olivia duck under before following suit.

"Agreed," she sighed. *What did you do, Simon Fisher?*

4

Lydia Fisher had been pulled into the lobby by Lawrence's lady friend by the time they ventured over to speak with her. She had light brown slightly greying hair and a rather pinched face. A gentle dusting of freckles painted her nose, and her grey eyes stayed glued to the ground, all but defeated. Her petite frame leaned against the hallway.

"Mrs. Fisher?" Olivia asked gently as they approached, giving a nod to the officer. After a moment, her eyes drifted up to briefly meet Olivia's. There was barely a register of acknowledgement before they returned to the floor.

"Oh, please, call me Lydia. That won't be my last name for long," she sighed.

The detectives exchanged a look.

"We're sorry for your loss, ma'am," Lawrence offered up.

"Don't be." Her voice was biting, aggressive, while also holding a note of defeat.

Olivia furrowed her brow.

"Did you have a strained relationship with your husband?" she asked, maintaining a steady watch of Lydia's face.

"That's one way of putting it," the woman scoffed.

Olivia glanced nervously over to Lawrence, who looked equally as puzzled.

"Would you care to elaborate?" She spoke the words carefully, making sure not to seem as though she was pressing too hard.

The woman rubbed at her arms.

"Could we, I mean, is there any way we can do this somewhere more private?" Lydia inquired, glancing about. She crossed her hands into her chest. "I know that the flat is a crime scene, but I'd also like to grab some of my things."

They were momentarily distracted by a group of gawking teenagers poised by the police cordon outside just to accentuate her request for privacy even more.

Olivia understood it, though. What happened here was an overly sensitive incident.

"Unfortunately," she sighed. "We can't take anything from the flat until it's been thoroughly examined by our team, and in regard to speaking privately, we could take you down to the station if you'd like, or we could go for a walk behind the building. You might know of somewhere quiet?"

Lydia slowly nodded, her eyes still on the floor. *She's in shock*, Olivia noted.

"There's a bench in the gardens," The woman replied, her voice lofty.

Lawrence glanced at her with a raised eyebrow. He most probably didn't think it was appropriate, but she wanted all the information while it was fresh on her mind and in a setting she felt most comfortable in.

"That's great," Olivia urged. "Sounds ideal. Then we can speak, just the three of us,"

Lydia nodded, peeling her body away from the wall and letting herself meet the detectives' gazes once again.

"This way," she muttered before leading the woman towards the building's entrance. Olivia let Lawrence step forward first to follow, holding herself back to speak with PC Reece.

"Did she see the body?" Olivia whispered.

"Yup," The young officer sighed. "And she didn't just see it. When we arrived on scene, she was just… standing over it." She was clearly uncomfortable at the recollection.

"But she wasn't the one who reported it?" Olivia asked.

"No, that was someone entirely different."

"Interesting," Olivia mused. "Listen, you've been a great help…Reece."

The name, even though most probably spelt differently, ached hearing it attached to someone else who had no idea how utterly fascinating her own Rhys was.

"Beth," the officer offered. "Just call me Beth." She reached her hand out instinctively.

"Well," Olivia replied, a smile breaking across her face. "Nice to *formally* meet you, Beth."

PC Reece shook Olivia's hand with an intense vigour. Clasping it tightly as though they were the closest friends already. With another, weaker smile, Olivia excused herself to follow after her partner and the deceased man's wife.

"You're going to have to call Beth," Olivia teased as she met up with Lawrence, who walked wordlessly behind Lydia by about five paces.

"You're on first name terms already?" Lawrence asked, alarm spreading across his features. Olivia stifled a laugh.

"Yes, and my hand may be bruised from our handshake," she replied. "But my advice? Either ask her out for a coffee or find a non-work time to gently let her down."

Lawrence shook his head.

"One other thing." Olivia lowered her voice; Lawrence instinctively drew closer. "Lydia was standing over the body when officers arrived on scene. Just…standing."

"She's definitely in some sort of shock," Lawrence observed, his voice barely above a whisper.

"Agreed. The only question is..." Olivia pondered, "...is that because she's seen her husband splayed across the ground like roadkill—"

"Or because she just killed someone for the first time in her life." Lawrence finished.

The thought settled on them both.

"She's awfully small to shove a man of Simon's height and weight off of a balcony, don't you think?" Olivia asked, sizing up the newly widowed woman.

"I've seen crazier things," Lawrence replied, causing Olivia to shrug. It was hard to disagree with that.

"We'll keep a close eye on her while we question her," she decided. "See if anything triggers her anger again or shocks her out of her current state."

Even though Lydia had said she knew where she was going, her body language read more like someone wandering through the hills than a woman with a specific destination. A chill that was not entirely due to the cold day rustled its way through Olivia's body.

"Agreed," Lawrence sighed. "You'll take the lead?"

Olivia nodded. They followed Mrs Fisher silently the rest of the way to the lone bench that sat facing the bleak apartment block, ready to make sense of it all.

5

"Here we are," Lydia called out, her voice again seeming to float into the air. She reminded Olivia of a vengeful ghost, untethered from the world except for her anger and sorrow.

The bench was a humble thing, cosied up under a tall ash tree. There was enough space for Lydia and one other person to sit; Olivia chose to rest on the opposite end of the bench, Lawrence standing a bit back in order to face the two women.

"Lydia, you seem to be in quite a bit of shock," Olivia observed as she settled on the bench beside her. "The officer told me that you saw your husband's body after he fell. That's a lot to process."

Lydia stared off into the distance, a warped laugh escaping her lips.

"It's okay to have complicated feelings about seeing him on the ground like that," Olivia offered, trying to break the ice a bit more. She let her head tilt as she spoke, her eyes intent on the woman in front of her who simply scoffed.

"Why were you so upset with him, Lydia?" She let her voice quiet as she asked, attempting to meet Lydia's unearthly tone.

"He's a high school teacher, you know?" she answered. "*Was* a high school teacher, I suppose. Taught English at the school down the road." Again, her voice seemed disembodied, just like her answer. "I work in A+E so I'd be home four nights a week then off for two. Rinse, recycle, repeat. We had a good life, all things considered." She seemed to catch herself at that last statement, as if she was bleeding her cards in a poker game.

"Until..." Olivia led on. *Let it out, Lydia*, she wanted to urge.

"He had an affair." Lydia spit out the words. Liv glanced up to Lawrence, who was hiding his rapt attention behind his notepad. He gave her a quick look before returning his eyes to Lydia.

"Having a partner cheat on you... That can be unforgivable," he replied.

Olivia studied her partner's face. She knew he had a difficult past, but she was too prudent to ask the specifics, and every once in a while, he let something new slip. Olivia just couldn't tell if this was one of those times or something fabricated to coax more information out of their witness.

"That's not the worst of it, though," Lydia replied.

Lawrence perked up an eyebrow.

"Well, can you tell us the worst of it?" Olivia coaxed.

The woman took a deep breath, almost as though she was trying to inhale the words about to break free.

"He..." she paused, composing herself. "I mean, it was a student he slept with. A bloody fifteen-year-old." Lydia's voice broke with that statement, tears springing forth as if out of nowhere. She buried her head in her hands, sobs wracking her back.

"I'm so sorry," Olivia replied, moving her hand to their witness's shoulder. She gave it a tentative squeeze. "I can't even begin to imagine..."

"Can't imagine, what?" Lydia shot back. "That you find out your husband of twelve years is a paedophile? No, I think not." Rage filled her voice this time. She was still in the midst of her grief over that pain—how could she possibly be ready to process the fact that her predator husband was now dead? Pieces were starting to click into place.

"Lydia, I can't imagine how difficult today is for you, you're right," Olivia agreed, keeping her tone low and steady to calm their witness down. "Thank you for taking the time to talk with us. We really appreciate it. I'm going to keep asking questions, but just let us know if you need a break." She paused, and when Lydia didn't seem to interrupt, she pressed forward. "When did you discover that Simon was…unfaithful?"

A man walking his dog crossed over behind them. He gave Olivia a polite nod.

Lydia didn't speak until he was well out of earshot.

"Just over a month ago," she replied, voice once more sinking into despair. "I knew something was going on for a while beforehand. You know when you just *know*? But I'd assumed it was another teacher, or maybe someone he met at a pub. Not—" Sobs overcame her ability to speak once again.

"That must have been a real shock to discover," Lawrence interjected. "Did anyone else know? Friends of yours, family?"

Lydia shrugged.

"I threatened to go public with it," she answered. "But I knew that wouldn't be fair to the child. I'm not even sure which kid it is. I tried to get him to tell me which one of his students it was, but he wouldn't budge on that."

Lawrence nodded as he made notes.

"And how'd you find out?" Olivia asked, again giving Lydia's arm an assuring squeeze. "How did you know it was with a student?"

"He told me," she cried. "He had had too much to drink one night, and I thought I could wrestle information of an affair out of him. I had no clue it would work. But then he broke down and told me he'd been dating one of his *students*." Lydia wailed at that statement.

Hastily, Lawrence procured a tissue.

"But he wouldn't say who it was?" Olivia searched Lydia's face.

The woman shook her head as she accepted Dean's tissue.

"Only that she was fifteen and that he knew it was wrong." She closed her eyes momentarily as though she was trying to conjure up the image of that conversation. "He said he was going to break it off with her, but I couldn't go back to sleeping in the same bed with him—sharing the same *space* with him—after that night. So, I packed a bag and went to stay with my sister across town."

Olivia nodded.

"No, I completely understand," she replied. "That would be hard for most people to come to terms with. And your sister, does she know why you moved out of your place?"

Lydia shook her head.

"Only that Simon and I were having a fight and that I didn't think we were going to be able to fix our marriage," she answered. "Margaret's a divorce lawyer, so she even offered to help me find good representation, but I knew that meant I'd have to talk about why I left him, and I just wasn't ready to tell other people yet."

Despite Lydia's disconnected stare and strangely disembodied voice, she seemed considerably more aware of her emotions than most people who'd just seen a mangled body. Olivia made a mental note of it. Was it because she had a lot of emotional maturity—or because she'd known that Simon would be vulture fodder that morning?

"Did you tell anyone else about it—a therapist? Maybe the school's Head?" Olivia asked.

"I should have but no. I spiralled after that night." Their witness locked eyes with Olivia. "I sunk into one of the worst depressions I've ever had. Called in sick at work, spent most days sleeping and most nights wishing I could stay asleep. I told myself that I'd come forward to the authorities, but to be honest I spent most of the time trying to drown out the knowledge that Simon had done something like that... *Could* do something like that." Lydia's eyes held an overwhelming sadness in them. Again, Olivia was reminded of a ghost.

"Did he try and contact you after you left?" she asked.

"Once or twice," Lydia sighed. "He left a couple of voicemails before I blocked his number. I couldn't face him again—" Her face crumpled at that statement, once again mourning.

"And last night, where were you?" Olivia asked.

The woman's eyebrows furrowed as she connected the dots and realised why they were asking.

"Goodness, I was at home with Margaret, like usual," she answered, displeasure still etched across her features. "I go to bed around nine these days, usually aided by a sleeping pill. Margaret woke me up this morning after she'd heard on the radio that there was a body found at the apartment building. I drove over—it was the first time I'd returned to the flat since I packed my bag. And when I saw Simon..." Her voice quieted, her eyes scanning the horizon rapidly. What was she searching for? Answers? Redemption?

"Margaret's your sister's name?" Lawrence asked, breaking his quiet observation. "Can we get her number from you? Nothing bad," he added when her eyes darted to him. "We'd just like to verify that you were indeed home."

She nodded easily.

"Of course."

Her words sent a chill through Olivia's spine. Clearly, she hadn't been concerned about Lawrence having the number. In fact, she almost appeared nonchalant.

Usually when they were so upfront about verifying alibis, people got defensive. Asked how they could possibly suspect *them* of having anything to do with someone's demise. Either that or they were overly generous about providing witnesses to their timeline. It was natural; people wanted to look good, and Lydia couldn't seem to care less that the detectives wanted to verify her whereabouts.

Olivia glanced at Lawrence to see if he'd noticed.

"Lydia... This may seem bold, so forgive me for asking it so bluntly. But did you kill your husband?" she startled herself with her upfront question. But maybe it would break through the veil of disillusionment that seemed to divorce Lydia from the rest of the world.

She turned, her grey eyes wide and yet somehow still far off, even as she met Olivia's gaze.

"No," she murmured gently. "I don't think so." Silent tears streamed down her face, two mirroring rivers.

"Thank you for your time, Lydia," Olivia sighed, giving her hand a squeeze. The new widow continued to look far off. "We'll get your contact information, as well as your sister Margaret's, and then we can have an officer drive you back to her place. Let us know if you need anything."

They wrapped up their meeting quickly with Lawrence stepping off to give Beth a call and describe where to meet the trio. Lydia continued to stare off, her gaze distant. Olivia couldn't shake it. She knew that shock manifested in many different ways, but she had a gut feeling that Lydia's wide grey eyes would haunt her at night until they found Simon's killer.

"Shall we?" Lawrence asked once Beth walked into sight. Olivia nodded, shoving her hands into her pockets as they marched off towards the apartment building.

"We'll be in touch, Lydia," she called over her shoulder. The small woman nodded once more.

Lawrence sighed as they walked out of earshot.

"That was one of the stranger interviews I've done with the spouse of a victim," he blurted out, looking to Liv. She nodded.

"Have you ever watched the ballet *Giselle*,

Lawrence?" The question bubbled to Olivia's mouth before she had much time to think about it.

"No, I can't say I have," he replied, curiosity reflecting in his eyes. "What's it about?"

"This village girl named Giselle," she relayed, "loves to dance, but she has a heart condition that means she shouldn't. Anyway, she falls for the wrong man—a liar. When she finds out who he truly is, it sends her into such a frenzy that her heart can't handle it. She dies in his arms." Olivia's gaze, much like Lydia's earlier, drifted off into the distance, grasping for something just out of sight.

"That's rather dark, don't you think?" Lawrence asked.

"That's only the first act," Liv replied, giving her partner a thoughtful look before gazing off into the unknown once more.

"What happens next?"

"She joins a group of ghosts called the Willis. They died virgins, scorned by men. They spend nights capturing men and forcing them to dance until they die." Images of white romantic tutus and dramatic lighting danced in Olivia's imagination.

"I retract my statement about Act I being dark," Lawrence laughed.

Olivia nudged him.

"Anyway, Albrecht, the guy who broke Giselle's heart," she continued, "he shows up to the forest the night she's reanimated as a Willis so that he can place flowers on her grave. The queen of the Willis wants to kill him—rightfully so in my opinion," Olivia added with a flourish.

"Ouch," Lawrence joked. "Remind me not to break any hearts."

She smiled at him.

"What's to say you haven't already?"

He nodded.

"Touché."

Liv pulled her coat tighter around her.

"Anyway." She nudged Lawrence again when he feigned exasperation at her story's continuation. "Giselle won't have it and pleads with the queen to spare Albrecht's life. Even after losing her life because of this man, she seeks salvation for him. She bears the burden of dancing through the night with him, and as day breaks and the Willis are banished from the earth until night returns, Albrecht lives to see another day." The wind whipped at their faces, filling in the gaps of their conversation.

"I didn't realise how wild some ballet stories were," Lawrence replied after a moment. "And as riveting as it sounds, what exactly does that have to do with Simon's death?"

Olivia stopped and turned to him. He followed suit.

"My question is," she answered. "Which one is Lydia? Giselle, the broken-hearted woman who will still find goodness in the man who scorned her? Or Myrtha, the ruthless queen with a harsh sense of justice?" She pondered the question as she looked out onto the Cornish countryside.

"Which one are you?"

The question surprised Olivia, who turned to look at Lawrence.

"I'm not sure I know." She knew the statement was true as she spoke it. "And if I'd found out that my husband of over a decade was abusing a teenager? All bets are off at that point."

"Agreed," Lawrence sighed. "I just hope we're able to figure out who his victim was."

"Me too." Simon Fisher had taken many dark secrets with him off the top of his balcony. Hopefully, they didn't become buried in his grave.

6

The flat was a disaster. If there had been any doubt about foul play based solely off the body, it was quickly squashed by the scene that unfolded before Olivia and Lawrence. Debris was strewn about the lounge—books and upended plants made the room look less like a living space and more like a recent tornado site. A coffee table lay on its side, shattered glass cluttering the floor around it.

"I guess we know where those lacerations came from," Lawrence breathed, noting the trace amounts of rust-coloured blood that were sprinkled over the glass. A couple of lab techs were swabbing for samples as they spoke.

"Maybe we'll get lucky and our killer was cut by the glass, too," Olivia hummed. She turned to Beth, who had joined them after escorting Lydia to another officer's car. Eagerness radiated off the young PC like a strong odour, bold and unyielding.

"How do people access the building?" Olivia asked.

"There's a key for the front door and another for each flat," Beth replied, her words flying out of her mouth. Olivia nodded.

"Any security cameras?" Lawrence inquired.

"They've got one in the lobby, but it's just for show. Building manager said it hasn't worked in over a year."

"So, we don't have a good way of establishing who's been in the building." Olivia sighed. "Have the officers who are canvassing also ask if residents noticed anyone besides the regulars walking the halls last night or early this morning. It's a long shot, but we might get something."

Beth's head bounced in a vigorous nod.

"This scene is violent. Whoever dispatched of Mr. Fisher was *angry*," Lawrence observed, pacing the lounge. The door to the balcony was still opened a fraction.

"Classic overkill," Olivia agreed. "And whoever it was didn't bother to clean up. Interesting if it happened early in the morning when the killer theoretically had the time to restore the apartment before anyone found the body and the police arrived."

"Does that mean anything to you?" Lawrence asked, walking over to a bookcase.

"Well thought-out killers usually feel the need to clean up after themselves," Olivia observed. She glanced to Lawrence. "It doesn't rule them out—just something to think about."

Lawrence flicked through the pages of a book before putting it back.

"Plus, Simon was a decent size. Easily at least 14 stones, don't you think?"

"At the very least," Olivia agreed.

"A hospital letter found on the worktop puts him at 13stone 11pounds," Beth chipped in. Olivia bit her bottom lip to stop herself from saying something sassy in return.

"And how tall?" Dean asked, oblivious.

"5ft 9," PC Reece replied.

Both detectives nodded.

"So," DI Lawrence mused. "The killer comes in through the doorway, manages to get Simon on the ground. He tortures him for a bit—throws him through the coffee table, strangles him for a little, trashes the apartment for dramatic effect. Once he's gotten enough rage out by beating up Simon, he realises it's not enough. He opens the balcony door and drags the man outside…" Lawrence walked over the broken glass and towards the slightly ajar balcony door as he described the scene. "He's able to either pick Simon up or incapacitate him enough that he can't struggle as he's pulled up onto the railing and then…"

"Splat," Olivia sighed, looking over the guardrail to see the cordon from the ground. A couple of evidence notes pointed out scuff marks on the balcony's flooring as well as on the rail. "Do you think he was able to put up a fight?" she asked, forcing herself to look away from the drop. Looking down from a height for too long made her feel strange.

"If he was," Lawrence answered, "It was pretty futile. Most of the destruction in the flat looks less like a struggle and more like a tantrum. Sure, maybe he fought back at the beginning, but if the attacker was able to choke him for long enough, he could've barely been conscious when he was tossed over the edge."

Olivia hummed in agreement.

"Beth, is there anything else of note in the flat?" she called out, looking towards the young constable. The PC brushed her hair back as she flounced over to the duo.

"His computer's clean—like wicked clean," she answered. "It wasn't locked and doesn't have any files on it or in the bin section. Either he was deleting stuff regularly or whoever came in made sure we couldn't find anything on it."

"That could be important—especially if he was indeed a paedophile," Olivia observed. Beth blanched at that comment.

"I'm sorry—he was a…a…?"

"Yes," Olivia sighed, cutting her off. "Or at least that's what he told his wife. He was apparently 'dating' one of his 15-year-old students, but it could have started when the girl was as young as 14. Sick is what I call that. In your mid-30s, no less." Olivia felt rage build behind her eyes the more she thought of it. "It means that it could have been Mr. Fisher or the assailant that wiped the hard drive. If he was a predator, he probably would have had some files on his computer. They normally do. But maybe he was sneakier about it. Less messy with his tracks."

"Anything else, dolly—er, Beth?" Lawrence's face deepened three shades of red as the nickname accidentally slipped past his lips. PC Reece's cheeks didn't fare much better either, though she quickly brushed it aside.

"Since you ask, *Detective*," she made sure to emphasise his role. "Forensics have found some fingerprints, but not as many as you might expect considering the crazy nature of the flat," she spoke quickly, trying not to fumble over her words.

"So maybe the killer wore gloves?" Lawrence replied, just as hastily.

Olivia let her lips break into a broad grin. A glance from her partner quickly shut it down. So there clearly had been something deep between the awkward pair in front of her.

She turned to survey the mess about them.

"This place seems like it was quite tidy besides the ruckus caused by the killer," Olivia observed. "Beth, you've been an excellent help. By the way, could you make sure to have forensics grab the bedsheets and test them for fluids. Mr. Fisher seemed to keep everything clean, but maybe he didn't do a good job of laundering his linens. We're going to need to figure out *who* his student victim was—the sooner, the better."

"Agreed," Lawrence chimed in. "That would be very helpful, *Beth*." It was his turn to overenunciated her name.

Rightly so, Olivia thought to herself. *Keep yourself focused on the job, Lawrence.*

"On it," PC Reece replied before practically jogging to the bedroom.

"She's one wired officer," Olivia noted as the brunette walked off.

Lawrence cleared his throat.

"Let's not forget that I can also tease you about Duracell," he returned. "I suggest you don't mention what you heard here again." His voice was almost a low growl, and Olivia couldn't hold back her laugh. His serious face amused her all the more.

"Your secret's safe with me, Dean," she reassured him, giving him an overexaggerated pat on the back.

"Thanks," he muttered.

"Well then, is there anything else you want to look at before we head back to the station?" Olivia asked, looking to toward the balcony one last time.

Lawrence nodded.

"Let's quickly glance in the bedroom and then we can be off," he replied, leading the way.

Olivia trailed behind him.

The room was similar to the rest of the flat—well-decorated, clean, tidy. Almost sparse without feeling like a bachelor pad. The queen-sized bed sat in the centre of the back wall; it was made, ready for Simon to return, though he never would.

Beth was stood beside the window talking to a forensic scientist, and on the side chest of drawers there was a photo of the victim smiling broadly with Lydia in his arms.

"He really was picky about his space," Olivia observed.

Lawrence nodded.

"I agree." He looked around him, purposefully avoiding the area where PC Reece was. "Even with his wife's absence, he clearly knew how to keep a place tidy. Maybe he had help?" He let the last comment hang for a moment. "Let's head back to the station."

"Agreed." She squeezed past the forensic team to lead their way back into the main room of the flat and gave it a once over before turning to the door.

"Anything else?"

Lawrence simply shook his head.

THE PAIR MADE their way quietly through the building and back into the lobby. Olivia noticed that even though there was clearly a police scene happening, none of the neighbours seemed overly eager to figure out what was happening in their building. *That's a bit odd*, Olivia thought to herself.

"Do you think it's strange we didn't deal with any

nosey neighbours?" Olivia asked as the duo exited the building.

"A bit, yeah," Lawrence answered. "Plus, it's not as though a splat like Simon's wouldn't have been loud. The fact that no one woke up to or heard the spectacular struggle that happened in the flat—or the fall itself—is puzzling."

"You know, the more people there are around, the less likely someone is to report something like a violent crime?" Olivia shared.

"Really?" Her partner asked, tilting his head to the side.

She nodded.

"Everyone thinks that someone else will take care of it. It's why if someone's having a heart attack, they teach you to designate someone specific to call for help. Otherwise, people will just stand and stare."

They made it to the car and both Lawrence and Olivia climbed inside.

"What's our plan?" Olivia asked. "Our next move?"

Lawrence put the key fob into the ignition but didn't start the engine.

"We head back to the station and see whatever records we can manage to find on Simon Fisher, as well as his wife. We can try and get in contact with the principal of his school as well. I'd like to keep the news out of the media until at least Monday; see if we can break the news to his students, see if we get any strong reactions."

Olivia nodded brusquely at that comment.

"Do you think it was someone related to his victim?" Dread filled her chest as she asked the question.

Lawrence looked at her.

"Well," he sighed. "If you were the parent of a teenager who just found out they'd been sleeping with their teacher, would you wait for the law to carry out justice? Or would you take it into your own hands?"

Olivia winced at the thought.

"Would make sense," she offered. "But, then there's Lydia..."

Her partner nodded with a frown.

"You're right," he agreed. "I say we confirm her alibi. And then we should get home at a decent hour tonight. I get the feeling we'll only be able to learn so much before we visit Simon's school."

Lawrence started the engine, animating the car to life. He gave her a look, which she returned in kind.

This one's going to be difficult.

7

The bright clack of Olivia's evening heels punctuated the detective pair's march down the hallway of Newquay Police Station. They had phoned Det Supt Collins on their way back from the flat where Simon Fisher had met his untimely end. Their boss had sighed when they informed him that Fisher in all likelihood had been sleeping with one of his students.

"Bastard," Collins had practically spat out of his mouth.

Olivia had sighed in agreement.

"We're going to rendezvous at the station to do some digging on him," she'd explained. "Hopefully, if he was hurting a kid, he got sloppy at some point."

Collins had given a lengthy pause.

"Feel free to call in Clara Fitzroy," he advised. "She's got some great insight as to how predators slink around the internet. Plus, I don't think she gets up to anything on Sunday afternoons."

"Right, sir," Olivia had replied, not wanting to mention that getting their tech analyst on board was already at the top of her list. "Clara would definitely be a huge help on this."

Collins had sighed, the weight of the weekend's work already weighing him down.

"Well, thank you both for the update." He sighed again. "Fisher sounds like someone who'd easily hold a target on his back. Losing his wife because he was caught having an affair with a student? That's three or four people who'd probably want him dead right there."

"It's going to be a rather large suspect pool, yes," Olivia had agreed. "Well, we're just about to arrive at the station. We'll pop over if there are any breaks."

He'd thanked them and ended the call before the detectives had had an opportunity to say anything more.

Detective Superintendent Steven Collins was a rather gruff man, and it had taken a while for Olivia to feel comfortable around him, although she most definitely admired him. And as she thought back to their conversations over the past few weeks, she couldn't help but feel as though she was starting to see the faintest of cracks in his façade. At the very least, she felt a sense of warmth when she realised that he did, in fact, trust her.

After the incident in London, she was convinced that no other police officer or detective would ever trust her again. After all, she'd survived something unimaginable while Rhys hadn't. And from her perspective, she should have done something else, something that would have ensured he made it through that day alive.

The first several months after the attack that left her without her partner and with three deep scars in her right side. She would lie in bed at night, trying to figure out what she could have done differently to save Rhys. It was her own personal chess game, rewinding and setting the pieces in a new motion, seeing if that fixed the problem. What if I had left at this point? What if Rhys had body armour on? What if we'd just kept on driving?

It became too difficult for her to maintain, though. The nightmares got scarier, her dependency on her pain medication rocketed, and it took an intervention from her sister, Mills, to recover from that spiral.

She'd broken down to her mandated therapist, telling him that she was just looking for a way that she could have changed the events of that day.

"You're trying to change the past, Olivia," he'd said, eyes full of an intense kind of sincerity. "You know that it's an impossibility, don't you?"

She had crumpled at that statement. But being forced to confront it, that no matter how hard she tried to save Rhys in her imagination, wouldn't change where she was today—without him.

Olivia shook out of her reverie, returning to the present moment of their investigation. She and Lawrence had made it back to their office space, which essentially was a small incident room with a few desks and computers. It housed their small team which included DC Harris but was missing a DS.

"Shit," Olivia breathed as they entered the room. Lawrence raised his eyebrow at her. "Earnest."

"Oh," he replied, realisation dawning on his face.

Olivia had fed him last night before the party, but her cat was probably irked that he hadn't been doted on yet.

"I'll give my mum a quick text," Olivia sighed, pulling out her phone. Lawrence nodded. *Case came up*, she typed as quickly as she could. *Could you swing by and feed Earnest and tell him he's the best?*

As she texted her mum, Lawrence wheeled out a fresh corkboard in front of their twin desks. Olivia sat down at hers once the message was sent, leaning back to look at her partner.

"Okay," he sighed. "What do we want to put on here?"

Olivia smirked. She knew that secretly, Lawrence was a big fan of finding the organisation to a case, placing all of the puzzle pieces on the board and seeing how they lined up.

"Let's start with Simon Fisher." Olivia sighed, cueing up his driver's license photo on her computer, ready to print at her partner's confirmation. Lawrence nodded. She glanced at his picture before clicking print; his dark eyes staring back. His hair was also dark, peppered with strands of grey. He seemed fit, although not outstanding in the looks department. Olivia shuddered as she thought about him trying to seduce a fifteen-year-old. "And of course, Lydia Fisher," she added, quickly finding the photo of Fisher's wife. It was of her on what appeared to be her graduation day and was taken by PC Reece at the flat and sent over. Her mouse clicked resolutely. Lydia's grey eyes reminded Olivia of the ocean—what depths did they hold?

"We don't know the name or identity of the student he'd been sleeping with, but she's definitely a part of this," Lawrence added, grabbing a sticky note and drawing a huge question mark and jotting below it 'abused student'.

"Agreed," Olivia nodded. "We should visit the Head tomorrow. Make sure that we can coordinate a notification at school that day or the day after."

Lawrence took a box of pins out of his drawer.

"Do you want to find the school's address while I get the board organised?" he asked, already moving to grab the two Fisher photos from the printer.

"Of course," Olivia replied, her eyes following her partner's movement to the main office. She waited for him to return. "You're very odd sometimes, you know?"

Lawrence waved a hand, not bothering to turn around.

"Nah, better hobby than some," he shot back, pinning the photos up. "You'll be thanking me for this later."

"You're probably right," Olivia agreed. She stopped

when the door to their office opened and Detective Constable Peter Epson came in with some papers.

"Sorry to interrupt," he breezed as he made his way over to Olivia. "I have some details for a Mr Stephen Hargraves. He's the headteacher of Simon Fisher's school and this is his home address."

Olivia took the papers, slightly surprised.

"Collins said you could do with the help as DC Harris wasn't able to come in and assist."

She offered him a smile.

"No, I mean this is great. Thank you. It saves me a job."

She looked over to Lawrence, who had momentarily stopped playing with his cork board.

"Nice one, Eppy." He nodded. "Great help!"

DC Epson left the room, and Olivia brought the address up on Google Maps.

"I say you turn up now," Lawrence suggested. "Why wait until tomorrow? Take the car."

Olivia was already standing, reaching for her coat on the hook.

"Way ahead of you on that one!" She pointed out with a smile. "I'll be back. Don't wait up."

8

Mr. Steven Hargraves' house was, simply put, a modest light bricked semi-detached new build on the outskirts of Newquay.

Olivia had made it over in record time, considering she was driving in heels and hadn't ventured out this way before.

She'd only had to ring the bell once, and moments later, the door swung open with a creak.

A large in height man with bright red tufts of hair and blue eyes opened it. His nose was crinkled upwards as though in a constant state of disapproval. He reminded her a lot of her own commanding head-teacher, who was more interested in being in control than actually checking in with her students.

"Bloody thing makes so much *noise*," he groaned with an exaggerated eye roll. "Sorry, can I help you?"

She heard the faint sound of children arguing inside as she held up her wallet and badge.

"Hello, I'm Detective Inspector Olivia Austin," she said slightly quieter than normal. "Is it possible to speak to a Mr Steven Hargraves, please?"

His expression changed from disapproval to wariness.

"Is this a joke?" he asked poking his head out of the door to look up and down his quiet cul-de-sac. "Can I have a look at the badge again, please?"

Olivia gave it to him.

"No joke I'm afraid, sir," she answered. He handed it back and she put it into her pocket, grateful that she'd listened to her CoLP colleagues previously who said to take it with you everywhere, even on nights out as you never knew when you might need it.

The man in front of her nodded slowly, satisfied that he wasn't the subject of an elaborate prank.

"I'm Steven," he said cautiously. "What's the matter? What happened? It's not my brother is it?"

Olivia paused.

"Is there somewhere private we can go?" she asked, glancing past his shoulder.

He thought for a moment, stepped out, and closed the door behind him.

"I've got a full house," he responded. "But please, what is all of this about?"

Olivia took her hands out of her pockets.

"Sir," she started. "I'm sorry to inform you that one of the teachers employed at your school, Newquay Tretherras, has passed away. His name was Simon Fisher."

She paused, attempting to gauge the reaction from the man in front of her.

"Simon," Mr. Hargraves exhaled. "Well, that's just unfortunate, isn't it? Thank you for letting me know."

He didn't seem all that distressed upon learning of his teacher's death.

"Mr. Hargraves," she continued. "We'd like to inform the whole school tomorrow, if that's all right with you?"

It was his turn to pause now.

"Do you think that's wise?" His voice sounded incredulous.

The blinds in the bay window beside them twitched. They now had an audience of little people.

"It could be paramount to the investigation," Olivia confirmed, keeping her expression stoic despite the small chubby face now pressed up against the window to her right. Little buggers.

"I suppose…" Mr Hargraves answered slowly, still not completely convinced. "I just worry about the students' well-being. That's quite a traumatic thing to tell them about on a Monday morning."

Olivia nodded.

"No, I completely understand your concerns," she soothed in her attempt to reassure the Head. "Don't worry, we'll arrange for there to be grief counsellors on site in the case that anyone feels the need to process such a tragedy. Plus, we can stay at the school for the rest of the day to provide additional support."

The door behind him opened, and a half naked toddler with a yoghurt-covered mouth giggled. And who she could only assume was *Mrs.* Hargraves appeared into view and stared at Olivia—confused for a moment, with one hand on her child's arm—before her husband closed the front door quickly.

"Sorry about that, Detective." He laughed awkwardly, and it was the first time she'd seen any real sense of warmth about him. "May I ask what exactly happened to Mr. Fisher that warrants a police investigation?" His voice had become somewhat solemn, grave and Olivia paused, working out how much she should divulge.

"Simon Fisher was found this morning," she answered, matching his grave tone. "Although there has yet to be a ruling as to the cause of his death, we have reason to believe that he was murdered." She kept her voice even as she spoke, doing her best to break the news gently.

"Tragic," Steven sighed.

"Indeed," Olivia agreed, unable to read his reaction. "Do you know of anyone who may have wanted to hurt Mr. Fisher? A teacher or student perhaps?"

The screwed up, disapproval nose came back.

"Unfortunately, I didn't know him too well," he said firmly. *Was that a touch of defensiveness?* "Although there had been a rumour recently that he and his wife had separated. Other than that, he's one of those teachers that flies under the radar; not so stellar that I often heard his praise, and not so abysmal that I needed to constantly lecture him."

Olivia made a mental note of that. *He doesn't know about the abuse, then.*

"So, he kept himself to himself..." she mused aloud. "Thank you for sharing that. Have there ever been any serious complaints lodged against Mr. Fisher during his time at your school?"

Steven Hargraves gave a small huff out at that comment.

"Fisher? The man was meek," he replied with a hint of surprise. "Forgive my bluntness, I just couldn't see him causing any real issue. All of our teachers will get complaints from time to time, but there wasn't anything of note against him that I can think of."

The confidence in Mr. Hargraves' voice made Olivia wince. *If only you knew.*

"I understand," she replied, measured. "Could you do me a favour when you get back into school?" she waited for him to nod. "Have a look into his records, see if there's anything of note?"

He paused again—whether for dramatic effect or because he was trying to decide, Olivia couldn't tell.

"It would be a shame for me to have to get a warrant, don't you think?" Olivia asked pointedly. That quickly spurred a cough from the Headteacher.

"Of course, I can find those files," he answered hastily. "There are some privacy laws that may mean I wouldn't be able to share all of the information with you, but I'll look into it."

She watched him glance up and down the street again. Clearly a man who cared a lot about keeping up with the Joneses.

"You do realise, Mr. Hargraves, that this is a murder investigation, correct?" Olivia did her best to hide the annoyance in her voice, although she was sure a hint of it seeped through. She paused, trying to see if the Head had anything else he felt compelled to add.

He rubbed the back of his neck.

"Yes, I understand," he said eventually. "You know, it's probably best that the students hear the news from an authority figure, now that I think of it. It would be awful for them to hear from all sorts of gossip and news stories. Yes, I'll call a school assembly for 9 a.m. sharp tomorrow morning." There was a certain heaviness to his voice as he said so.

"Thank you, Mr Hargraves." Olivia was pleased she'd managed to make him warm to the idea. "I'll be there, along with my partner, Detective Inspector Lawrence. We'll make sure we're discreet and respectful."

"You can call me Steven when it's just us, Detective," he replied. "Thank you for coming round to talk. I'll see you tomorrow."

"Likewise." Olivia exhaled as she watched the Headteacher in front of her open his door and disappear behind it.

She made her way back to the car, satisfied at the

confirmation that she and Lawrence would be able to go in. She had a feeling that the principal might not be the most forthcoming person—or the most in the know, for that matter. Still, she couldn't deny the assembly would be helpful.

Back in the confines of the car, Olivia called Lawrence, who was still most probably fiddling with his board.

"So, what do we think?" he asked. She could hear paper rustling in the background.

"He doesn't seem to know much," she mused in reply, running a hand through her by now wayward hair. Her eyes tracked a woman walking a dog briskly. "We should coordinate with some counsellors to meet at the school tomorrow then call Clara before we finish for the evening. I can't stop thinking about a glass of wine."

Lawrence laughed.

"Agreed," he confirmed. "I can call Clara?"

Olivia checked her watch.

"Don't worry, I'll do it if you want to call the counsellors?" She knew that Lawrence had some connections with the team they'd bring in. Distracted, she heard him mumble his agreement.

"Perfect." Liv sighed. "Let's get this organised so we can go home." It was nearing 3 p.m., and she wanted to eat dinner sooner rather than later. Plus, the office felt so empty on a Sunday. Most detectives worked from home if they could on the weekend.

Ending the call, she dialled Clara's number and sat back.

Clara, always the faithful worker, picked up midway through the third ring.

"Liv!" she squealed from the phone, almost loud enough that Olivia worried for her ear drum health.

"Hi!" Olivia couldn't help her grin. The 26-year-old tech analyst had a certain enthusiasm for life that never seemed to slow down. "How has your weekend been?"

She knew she was probably worse for wear like herself earlier in the morning.

"To be completely honest?" The young analyst groaned, though still managing to sound upbeat. "I've got the most wicked hangover after Susan's party,"

Olivia laughed. She clearly remembered Clara being an immovable force beside the bar.

"I'm not surprised," she observed. "Though I didn't realise you knew Susan." Usually, the IT team weren't very present with the police parties. "But it was nice to see you!"

Clara had worn a lovely blush pink dress with very tall silver heels. It was one of the few things that Olivia remembered from the foggy night before she had downed too many glasses of whatever was on hand.

"Oh, I was with a date," she answered, swallowing whatever she'd been eating. "Have you met Diana? Diana Hershel."

Olivia was grateful she didn't have a cup of tea to sip on; if she had, she certainly would have spit it out.

"PC Hershel?" she asked, doing her best not to sound incredulous.

"Oh, yeah!" Clara explained either oblivious to Olivia's surprised reaction or ignoring it... "She's great. I don't know if we'll go on many more dates, but it was nice to spend some time with her for the evening."

"Well, that's…exciting, isn't it?" Olivia muttered, doing her best to recover from her initial shock. A light smile found its way to her lips; they did seem like a sweet couple, once she thought about it. As she pondered the thought, she realised she'd only seen Clara in person a handful of times. Nonetheless, the bubbly, shorter-than-average tech analyst with chestnut-coloured skin and long box braids seemed like she'd be a good complement for Hershel, square-shaped glasses and all. Hershel's lankiness and freckled skin probably complemented Clara quite well.

"I always enjoy getting all dressed up," the young analyst admitted, her voice dreamy. Olivia grinned. "But we haven't called to gossip about work parties, now have we? How can I help you?"

She could have spoken to her about it for much longer, but alas, that glass of wine in the fridge at home wasn't going to pour itself.

"Well…" Olivia sighed. "As much as I enjoy catching up with you, did you hear about the murder from this morning?"

There was a brief pause and more sounds of chewing.

"Only a couple of details," she answered. "A man was beaten up and then found after having fallen off the side of his flat, correct?"

Olivia chewed her bottom lip in amusement.

"That's impressive for only catching a few details," she observed.

Clara laughed despite the grave topic.

"I like to stay up to date even if I haven't been called in already." More chewing. "God knows this department relies on me to know everything at all times."

Olivia could practically see Clara rolling her eyes.

"His name was Simon Fisher, right?"

"You're a genius," Liv said. "Spot on."

She could hear the sounds of fingers tapping away on a computer.

"Perfect," Clara said after a moment. "I've got a file prepped for you; I can send it straight to the printer at the station if you'd like? That is where you are, I'm assuming? Though I'm getting the vibe it's not..."

Olivia took her phone away from her ear to look at the screen.

"Damnit, Clara. Are you sure you aren't tracking my phone or something?" she joked. "Because if not, you're free to take over my job as Detective Inspector. You've clearly got awareness in spades."

Laughter pealed from the other end of the phone.

"Just a good sense for habits, I suppose," Clara admitted. "I'd be a rubbish detective, for the record. But the online analysis? I've got that down to an art."

"Indeed, you have," Olivia agreed. "There is one other thing, if I haven't overloaded you already. And this one isn't as pleasant, unfortunately." She sighed, tucking her hair behind her ear. "We have reason to believe that Mr. Fisher was involved with a fifteen-year-old student—"

"Fuck that!" Clara exclaimed, cutting off Olivia's thought.

She winced.

"Yes, it's awful," Olivia admitted. "But we think it's important that we figure out the identity of the girl he was preying upon. That might be the break that this case needs."

More fingers on a keyboard.

"Yes, that makes sense. I'll see what I can dig up. Although I have to warn you, Liv. Usually when a predator is abusing a child, they do their best to hide their tracks. I have some tricks up my sleeve, but it really depends on how sloppy he was," Clara admitted. "Still, I think the crime scene team recovered his phone, so that'll help with some initial digging."

Olivia smiled.

"You're incredible, Clara, honestly," she reminded her. "Thank you so much for sending that file over."

"What else are my Sundays for?" The tech analyst laughed.

Olivia couldn't quite tell whether Clara was joking or actually quite okay with doing some extra work on her day off. She seemed like the kind of woman who was married to her job. But then again, maybe that was more out of necessity than want.

"Oh, also," Liv winced as she said it, knowing that she'd already asked a lot. "If you could do some digging on his wife, Lydia Fisher, that would be absolutely great. You could always make someone else do that one for you though."

"Already done and sent over with Simon's files," Clara declared. "And I sent two copies, one for both you and Lawrence."

"Wow! I owe you a drink when this case is over. Thank you."

Clara laughed.

"You better be serious about that," she insisted.

"Wouldn't have said it otherwise," Olivia replied with a smile.

"Brilliant. I'll look forward to it, then," the tech analyst admitted, more sincerity in her voice than Olivia had been expecting. It caught her off guard. She registered that perhaps she wasn't the only one in the Devon and Cornwall Police Constabulary who may be in desperate need of a friend—outside of her partner and family of course. But she was stuck with Lawrence whether or not she wanted to be. Same with Mills and her mum. But Clara? She quite liked the idea of developing a true friendship with the woman, upon further reflection.

"Likewise." She smiled, warmth spreading over her features. "Okay, I'd like to get out of this car and get home in time to make myself dinner. I'll speak with you soon, Clara. Thanks again."

The bubbly analyst hummed in agreement before ending the call.

Olivia smiled to herself before starting the engine and embarking on her journey back to Newquay police station.

"Bloody brilliant," Liv found herself whispering as she approached the printer on her return. It shouldn't have surprised her that Clara had found an abundance of information on Simon Fisher, but she still balked a bit at the stack that awaited her. "Guess we get to pore over these late into the night," she sighed, glancing over to Lawrence, who had just put the phone down.

He shook his head at the pile.

"I'm glad you're back," he sighed. "I feel extremely good about calling this a night if you do."

Olivia put some of the papers down on Dean's desk.

"I don't know how much more we can get done here," she agreed, trying not to show her eagerness to get home to her cottage and put the fire on. Earnest was probably riled out of his mind by now, although her mum had sent her a text that she'd headed over and found him disgruntled but overall okay.

"Great. I can pick you up at eight tomorrow morning," Lawrence offered, stuffing his portion of the intense packet from Clara into his bag. "Then we can discuss how we want to handle notification to the school on our way over."

"That sounds brilliant," Olivia replied, grabbing her own set of information to bring home. She switched off her computer. "Right then, I'll see you tomorrow!"

She was almost out of their office when she heard her partner's voice.

"I guess you need a lift home, too," he observed with a smirk.

"Shit, I completely forgot." Olivia's eyes widened as she processed that not only had she not driven to work of her own accord, but she also still had the pair of increasingly painful heels on. It'd been a long day; there was no doubt about that.

"No worries," Lawrence laughed. "I'm happy to drive you," he confessed, putting his coat on with one swift movement.

"Thank you." Olivia waited by the door looking at the sea of empty desks in the main office. Even DC Epson had disappeared, though she could see Collins light was still on. "It's been a bloody long day."

"Agreed," Lawrence sighed. "Let's go home."

9

"Code red! Officer down!"

She was back inside the dream. It was different this time, though. Something felt... off.

She knelt down beside Rhys, his fingers pressed against young PC Jacobson's neck. He didn't look good. Blood was everywhere. And even though it was clearly a dream, Olivia already knew she couldn't do anything to stop the series of events that would come next.

"Fuck, we need that back up, like yesterday!" Rhys growled. His eyebrows were furrowed as he urgently tried to stem the spurting. "They've left us here like sitting ducks!"

Again, that sense of realisation dawned on her.

"It has to be us," she hissed, feeling rehearsed as the words tumbled out of her mouth. "We can't wait! The public need us. They need someone on scene!"

The words felt unreal even as she continued to speak them. What was she even saying?

The echo of ricocheting bullets pierced her eardrums, adding to the chaos of the scene. Make it stop, she willed herself. But a dark part of her needed to see the events play out. She needed to see it again. She needed to see that last look he gave her.

She met his eyes. *Rhys*, she wanted to call out. *Let's just leave. Get out while we still have a chance.*

If she'd said that, would he still be here now? She didn't care about all the honour and praise he'd received posthumously. Having him physically beside her meant more than that. It meant more than medals and certificates in a keepsake box.

If they'd stayed back, stayed out, they wouldn't have been heroes. But they would have had each other.

"No!" Rhys protested. Ever her protector. "*You* have to stay until they get here. They're on their way."

She pulled herself to standing. Screams orchestrated the dream, just as real as they had been on the actual day. Not just screams of fear and terror. Blood curdling screams. The type that's expelled from you when a bullet or two is plunged into your body. The dying kind.

"I'm going," she answered, feeling hollow but defiant. "I have to. I can't sit here and do nothing. Stay with Jacobson…" Those last three words. The worst ones she'd ever spoken. The three words that haunted her night after night. *Stay with Jacobson.*

Rhys grabbed hold of her arm tightly before she

could run off. Even in the urgency of it all, she still relished in his touch. It still made her feel safe and secure despite their surrounding chaos.

"*You* stay here!" he ordered. "Keep pressure on his neck until the ambulance arrives and I'll go. I'm not losing you today!" The whole thing felt like a twisted play. Who was the audience?

The bomb exploded, forcing Olivia to turn. This is it, she told herself. The point of no return. The screams got worse. The begging, the pleading. They needed the authorities on scene. Why had the backup taken so long to arrive?

"When the ambulance gets here, find me. I'm going along Poland Street!" *Tell him you love him. That you always will.*

But she was powerless against the force of the dream.

As she ran to meet the officers who descended on scene, she was met with a commotion unlike she had in dreams past.

"What?" she started to mumble out, breaking the cadence of the perfectly choreographed nightmare.

Out of nowhere, a shroud was pulled over her eyes, obscuring her vision in white tulle.

"Stop!" Olivia shrieked, clawing at the air, desperately trying to pull off the strange veil. But nothing would take it away.

She couldn't see him.

"Rhys!" she screamed, panic rising in her voice.

Rhys!

WAKING up from the nightmare was like trying to break to the ocean's surface while being chained to an anchor. Olivia pushed up and up, seeking escape. Slowly, she dragged herself into consciousness.

A gasp erupted from her lips, breaking through as her eyes burst open.

"*Fuck*," she groaned. Her heart was still pounding, her breathing laboured.

She sighed as she rolled over to her side, checking her clock for the time. 6:12 a.m. Could have been worse.

She lay in bed a minute longer, focusing on taking in deep breaths like her therapist had taught her. Her body slowly relaxed, releasing its tight grip on its fight or flight instinct.

Once she felt calm enough, Olivia swung her legs over the side of her bed to hop down and tread over to the bathroom sink. A splash of cold water to the face helped bring her further into reality.

She glanced up to see Earnest's eyes peeking at her from the mirror. She gave him a smile and turned to face him. He'd certainly given her a bit of the cold shoulder for abandoning him the night before, but after a fair amount of affection and praise, he had begrudgingly calmed down.

"I'm okay," she promised him, bending down to

scratch him behind the ears. His tail swished. "Just a bad dream."

OLIVIA FINISHED her breakfast and coffee just in time to meet Lawrence outside her cottage at 8:03 a.m. Despite getting an early start to the day, everything felt like it had a slight haze to it, as though the shroud that encased her in her dream still lingered during the daytime. She shivered as she thought about it, quickly walking down the path to Lawrence's car, hands shoved deep in her pockets. It was a bitter morning, that she was certain of.

"Sleep well?" Lawrence asked as she opened the door and squeezed herself into the seat.

She looked at him.

"You're joking, aren't you?" she scoffed, snapping Lawrence out of his lackadaisical reverie.

"Oh!" he responded, eyes widening. "Sorry, I assumed—"

"Yeah—assumed being the key word," Olivia interrupted, closing the door with a decisive thud. She hid the rush of blood to her cheeks, well aware that he had nothing to do with her bad start. It was most probably hormonal. She was almost certain the vivid dream was due to it being *that time of the month*.

"My apologies." Lawrence sighed, starting the engine with the turn of his keys. He paused for a moment. "Do you want to talk about it?"

Olivia felt rather than saw his eyes on her.

"Not particularly," she replied, resigned by the fact that no matter how bad she felt, telling her partner that only a couple of hours ago she'd been revisiting the tragic death of Rhys for the umpteenth time was a no-go. Would he have sent her back home? Told her to take the rest of the day off? "If it's all the same to you, I'd rather just focus on the case."

Lawrence cleared his throat, reading the room.

"Of course," he answered, voice almost defeated. "Right, were you able to read everything Clara sent our way last night?"

Olivia nodded, pleased for the subject change.

"I definitely gave everything a skim." She looked out the window, her eyes following the curve of the landscape as they drove. "I read the most important bits thoroughly, though. Simon Fisher seemed like a relatively average guy. Nothing but a couple of parking tickets on his police record, fairly mediocre university reviews, and a couple of begrudging students who gave him poor reviews online, although most seemed ambivalent on him."

Lawrence took one hand off the wheel to run it through his dark hair.

"It tracks with what Principal Hargraves said about him," he agreed, scanning the road. "Which makes me think that whoever he was abusing, it could have been his first time—maybe even the first time he decided to step outside of his marriage."

"That would make sense," Olivia concurred. "Lydia

mentioned having a sense about it. My guess is she'd have noticed earlier if he'd been making a common practice out of it."

Lawrence nodded.

"Nothing was particularly striking about Lydia's information, either," he observed.

She saw him turn to glance at her before facing the road again.

"Agreed," she mused. "By all outside accounts, they seemed like a perfectly normal couple," she mused. "It's weird how easily something so insidious can hide behind normality."

"Oh, are you a poet now, Austin?" Lawrence's voice was playful, the corner of his lips perked the slightest bit.

Olivia felt the ice that had coated her since she'd woken up from the nightmare slowly start to thaw. It was impossible to stay in such a downcast mood when her partner clearly hadn't given up on her.

"He was an English teacher, correct?" she continued, and Lawrence didn't appear wounded by her non-acknowledgement of his little jab at her.

"Correct," he answered. "Specialised in *Medieval English* while at uni."

Olivia could hear a hint of amusement in his voice.

"Maybe he used his work in English to attempt to seduce his victim." Olivia sighed. "These kids... They're so *impressionable* at that age. Teachers like Fisher should be protecting them, not preying upon them."

Lawrence's knuckles tightened on the steering wheel. Olivia could feel something building up in her partner. She fell silent, letting him decide when to let it out into the open.

"Is it terrible that I don't feel that bad that he's gone?" he asked.

The question punctuated the air, changing the whole moment. Olivia looked over to her partner. Despite his thirty years of age, he was newer to the career of a Detective than she was. He harboured passion and depth in every case that had Collins singing his praises to anyone that would listen, but as she looked at him, she saw the struggle he kept inside. The part that fought to separate his morals from his job. Everyone whether in uniform or not had a bout of that.

"So long as it doesn't interfere with your ability to find his killer and execute the law?" she answered. "No. Not at all."

Olivia didn't look to Lawrence as she spoke, but she hoped that he understood the gravity of her words.

"I've never…" Lawrence trailed off.

"I know," Olivia replied, finally looking at her partner again. "It's okay to be confused about it. My advice?" She settled her head into her hand to lean back further and really look at Lawrence. Conflict was strewn across his face. The desire to do good—and the confusion at what that truly meant. "If you're really conflicted, see Collins once the case is over. He'll help you sort out what you're feeling."

Silence came over the car, and after a brief moment, Dean spoke.

"Does it help?" he asked, his voice apprehensive. "Does talking about things *really* help?"

Did it? That was a good question. She'd done it a lot over the past year and a half. She'd opened up every corner of her mind to someone who started out as a stranger, but by the end of her sessions, her therapist had become her lifeline. It helped to turn on the tap of her thoughts and not stop until it was all out. That in itself meant the entire world to her. But this deep a conversation was for another time. She didn't want to go there. Not now.

Instead, she simply just nodded. Her response hung in the air.

"Okay," Lawrence sighed. He understood the timing wasn't right and proceeded to change the subject. "Well. How do we want to handle notifying the whole school that Fisher has passed?"

"Great question," Olivia replied, hoping that her partner felt okay with the change in depth. They'd go over it again later. "I've actually got a couple of ideas."

The hum of the car's engine, quiet and steady, stayed with the duo the rest of the drive, filling in those quiet moments where they just needed to sit and listen.

10

The crowd of unruly high school students teemed with life, almost its own living organism with its own set of rules and patterns. Olivia had observed the hallway as Mr Hargraves made an announcement over the PA system that the school was going to have an assembly in the main hall. Kids had flocked from every crevice of the school into a wave of navy and black uniforms, whispers and the click of shoes accompanying their movement towards the aforementioned meeting place.

Olivia had quickly ducked into the main office before the assembly began, checking in with the woman at the front desk.

"This is my email address. Could you send me a list of every student who doesn't end up coming to school today?" Olivia asked, sliding her card across to the matronly woman, who wordlessly nodded before resuming her task for the day.

"I'll also need a list of every student who was born in 2004 or 2005," Olivia explained, trying to make eye contact with the woman. "And every student enrolled in Mr. Fisher's classes the past two years."

"Got it," the receptionist responded, finally looking up at Olivia rather impatiently.

"Thank you," Olivia replied, knocking on the desk before exiting the office.

Olivia felt good about the way she and Lawrence had arranged for the assembly to go. A couple of uniformed police officers had discreetly set up at the school's main exits in case anyone left before Olivia and Lawrence could identify them. The two had a solid plan as to how to proceed forward.

Now, Olivia stood towards the back of the stage in the hall, Lawrence by her side. The sea of teenagers settled only after Hargraves rather aggressively tapped the microphone connected to the podium he stood at.

"Good morning, students and staff alike. I hope you all have had a good weekend. I have some guests here with me this morning who would like to speak with you on an…important matter," Hargraves soliloquised to the crowd, seemingly a bit unsure with how to introduce the detectives despite clearly having notecards in front of him.

His hands gripped and released the sides of the podium he stood at. His bright red hair stuck straight out of his head, an even brighter beard drawing attention away from the bald spot atop his crown. His large height meant he had to hunch over the podium somewhat. He certainly gave off the impression that he was simply put, a gentle giant. Perhaps it was an act—though for now, he didn't give any reason to think otherwise.

"So, without any further ado," he continued, "I'd like to hand this meeting over to Detective Inspector Lawrence."

The crowd stirred at the mention of a detective. A couple of students tried to stand, seemingly to skirt out of the auditorium, but teachers quickly had them sit back down, and Olivia made a mental note of them.

Lawrence, however, looked incredibly nervous as he stepped forward towards the podium. He looked professional enough, what with his black tailored trousers, white shirt and skinny black tie. His black suit jacket seemed to weigh him down under the bright lights of the stage, and Olivia was struck by the fact that he was indeed quite stiff. He cleared his throat as he looked out into the audience of teenagers. Olivia wanted to coax him forward slightly more, encourage him that he was doing a good job. Instead, she just let herself watch the crowd, keeping an eye out for any anomalies.

"Uh, hello everyone," Lawrence spoke, leaning into the microphone. A couple of snickers echoed throughout the hall. Otherwise, everything was perfectly still. The calm before the storm, Olivia thought to herself.

"I'm here today with my partner, Detective Inspector Austin." Lawrence gestured back to Liv, who kept her eyes firmly scanning the crowd, arms crossed. "We're here because we have some unfortunate news to share with you all." He paused to set the intrigue. "Over the weekend, one of your teachers, Simon Fisher, sadly passed away."

The hall was still for a split second as the crowd processed the news. Before the quiet could fully settle, sound and movement erupted seemingly from every which way. Some teens yelled "what?" while others laughed. Whether it was out of disdain for Mr. Fisher or disbelief that something had happened to him, she couldn't be sure. Even more students turned to their friends, the shock in their eyes clear even from Olivia's perspective on the stage.

Olivia noticed a blonde-haired girl towards the back wall after a moment of reflection. Her friend hugged her shoulders tightly, seemingly speaking words of reassurance, although the blonde girl seemed utterly inconsolable. Another girl with dark brown hair stood up and rushed past one of the teachers guarding the hall. Before the teacher could stop her, she had slipped out, anger written plainly on her face.

An athletic-looking boy stood up and practically spat out the word "good!" The crowd burst into more noise at that. While some of the teachers seemed a bit upset, they all maintained impressive composure.

"Students, *please*," Lawrence practically yelled into

the microphone. "A moment of your time." The ruckus calmed to a murmur. "I understand that this can be deeply upsetting news, especially if you've had Mr. Fisher as a teacher." The crowd was giving Lawrence more and more of their attention. *Good job, partner,* Olivia wanted to call out.

"There are some grief counsellors who have come to the school today. If you feel like you need to speak with a professional, please feel free to schedule an appointment with one of them." The crowd was nearly silent at that. "Additionally, if you feel you have any information about Mr. Fisher, DI Austin and I will be at the school for most of the day and are happy to meet with you. We'll also post the number you can call if you'd like to report anything anonymously. Your privacy and confidentiality will absolutely be our utmost priority." Lawrence had evened himself out after his shaky introduction, that was certain.

"How'd he die?" a boy called out from the crowd.

"The medical examiner has not ruled on Mr Fisher's death yet," he replied, ever the diplomat. "That being said, we're treating his death as suspicious. Past that, I am not able to comment."

The crowd was getting out of hand again. More teens were crying, and a fair number seemed to become belligerent.

"Detective Austin and I will be set up in Room 207, one of the IT rooms, throughout the day. Again, please *do not* hesitate to reach out, either to us or any of the grief counsellors. Thank you all for your time," Lawrence wrapped up, stepping back from the podium so that Principal Hargraves could attempt to quell their audience. Students were starting to stand in large droves though, ready to escape the claustrophobic hall.

"Great job, partner," Olivia muttered as she and Lawrence exited out the back of the stage.

"You're just saying that," Lawrence shot back, wringing his hands.

"I'm not," Olivia assured him. They quickly headed down the back hallway, towards the room Principal Hargraves had set up as their home base of operations for the day. "Teenagers are difficult. You managed to wrangle an unruly crowd and do it with grace. Seriously." She made a point to look intensely at Lawrence with that last statement.

He sighed.

"Kids exhaust the fuck out of me." He sighed again, wiping his hands against his trousers.

"You and me both, Lawrence." Olivia chuckled. "Lucky for us, we get to spend the rest of the day surrounded by them."

11

It had been an exhausting day of interviews. An initial rush of students eager to speak had bolted from the hall to the makeshift interview room, resulting in a line halfway down the corridor. Most of them just wanted to tell the detectives something they already knew—Mr. Fisher was on the 'outs' with his wife, or he was practically to the point of insignificance within the school community. Olivia got the sense that mostly they just wanted to feel like they were involved in some way. It made sense, really; it was a perfectly natural response to learning of a questionable death.

A couple of teens mentioned other peers who struggled in Mr. Fisher's class. There was one student who had apparently made a somewhat vague threat to him during class, although Olivia was sceptical that a tiff in the classroom warranted stalking Simon to his flat and committing such intense overkill. It was hard to tell, though, so they still wrote his name down.

Before they had commenced interviews, Olivia took a moment to phone Hargraves and ask him about the three students she had noticed in the immediate aftermath of the news breaking: the crying blonde girl, the brunette who had stormed off, and the idiot who'd yelled 'good' at the news of Fisher's demise. Hargraves immediately assured Olivia that he would track them down and send them to Olivia and Lawrence. He also promised to bring the information that she had requested from the secretary.

The boy was brought in first. Hargraves practically shoved him into the room then bolted over to Olivia to drop a manila folder before leaving, giving the teen one last warning glare.

From the corner of the room, the appropriate adult, a woman called Bev, braced herself for unruly behaviour.

The shouter had a mop of blonde hair atop his pretty face and cocky blue eyes like no one else. He leaned against the back wall, facing the detectives without engaging. Olivia eyed him closely.

"What's your name?" Lawrence asked after Hargraves had left the room. The boy sulked in the back of the room, his arms crossed. "I'll wait."

"Harry," he responded eventually. He wouldn't make eye contact with either detective.

"Harry..." Olivia coaxed, looking up expectantly from her notepad.

"Price." He sighed. "Harry Price."

"Well, Harry Price, it's nice to meet you. Thank you for coming," Lawrence spoke. He gestured to the chair across from himself and Olivia. "I'd like to introduce Bev over here. She's just going to make sure you're okay. Please. Have a seat."

"I'd rather not," Harry grumbled.

"Suit yourself," Lawrence sighed.

"So, Harry, have you ever had Mr. Fisher as a teacher?" Olivia asked. She figured it was a good warmup question. The boy shook his head.

"Really?" Olivia let scepticism coat her words. "Because I saw and heard you shout 'good' when you learned that Mr. Fisher had passed away. Would you like to explain that?"

The boy was shifting back and forth, trying to figure out a configuration that would make him comfortable. They sat in silence for a moment, Olivia giving him time to decide if he wanted to answer.

"Will you please answer the question, Harry?" Lawrence asked.

"I—" Harry started, but the word died in his throat before he could finish it.

"You what?" Olivia asked, mimicking Harry's crossed arms. It was one of her favourite interview techniques: mirror the person you're speaking with so that they feel more inclined to speak with you. "C'mon, there's got to be a good reason for a kid like you to be happy a man's dead."

He glanced at Bev, who nodded gently.

"I'm *not* a kid," Harry protested, his eyebrows furrowed. Olivia knew his type too well. The popular boy. The kind who was good at everything, never short of female attention, and most probably the class joker. If only they could see him now.

"Really?" Lawrence pushed without getting too aggressive. Smart. "How old are you then?"

"Seventeen," Harry retorted, puffing his chest a bit. "And I said 'good' because I meant it. I'm glad the bastard's dead."

The detectives exchanged looks. So, he was a sixth former. That explained the lack of uniform.

"Why is that, Harry?" Olivia coaxed. "Obviously, you want someone to know that you don't like Mr. Fisher, otherwise, you wouldn't have made such a show back in the hall."

The three of them looked at each other as Olivia's words sunk in. Harry glanced to the detectives directly for the first time since entering the room before hunching back into his casual pose against the wall. *You're scared*, Olivia wanted to say. Everything in his body language suggested an intense nervousness. He was masking it in nonchalance, but even from a distance, she could tell that his breathing had quickened since Hargraves had deposited him in the room.

"You can't tell her that I told you," Harry half whispered, craning his neck to peer above the detectives. He was practically squirming. *Her?* Olivia gave Lawrence another look. He met her glance in perfect synchronicity.

"Well, Harry, that depends on what you're about to share with us," Olivia explained cautiously. "We can do our best to be discreet, but if it's a matter of physical safety, I can't make promises that we won't contact anyone else regarding the matter."

"It's a safe space to talk," Bev piped up, leaning forward on her chair.

Harry bounced his back against the wall, drumming the drywall with his palm.

"Please, Harry," Lawrence urged. "If he hurt someone you know, you need to tell us so we can help her heal."

Harry's eyes shot to meet with Dean's as the detective spoke.

"What do you know about Mr. Fisher hurting anyone?" the teen asked, voice suddenly a bit higher. He sounded alarmed as he asked. He'd been trying to hide something, but Lawrence and Olivia had found it.

"That it's possible that Mr. Fisher wasn't the great relaxed teacher that everyone thought he was," Lawrence replied, trying to stay vague.

Harry cleared his throat.

"Well. You should know…" He was struggling to find the words. "My sister, Emma, she had him as a teacher."

Olivia gave Lawrence a side glance before jotting

Emma Price in her notepad. Could this be the lead they needed in the case?

"Did Fisher hurt your sister, Harry?" Olivia focused her eyes on the boy as she asked. He still did his best to avoid her gaze.

"No. Well... Kind of. She definitely got some weird vibes from him when she was in year 11," Harry started to explain. "See, Emma doesn't do reading too well; she's dyslexic. At first, Fisher was great about helping her with her schoolwork, making sure she didn't fall behind and whatnot. She's always relieved when she finds a good teacher like that. Until..." Alex cleared his throat again, rubbing the back of his neck with his hand.

"Did he try something?" Lawrence asked.

Olivia glanced to her partner. Don't lead him too much, she wanted to urge him. Still, she could tell that Harry was still hesitant to talk more.

"He offered to help her study on a Saturday. Gave her an address, only—only it was his place, you see?" Harry explained.

Olivia tried her best not to let her jaw open. Was Simon Fisher really so bold as to blatantly invite a student to his flat?

"As soon as she realised that it wasn't a library or a coffee shop, she scarpered the hell away from there. He tried to act like it wasn't anything weird, but Emma knew that he was covering his arse too hard for someone with innocent intentions." Harry had transitioned to cupping his eyes in his palm, rubbing slow concentric circles into them.

"I'm so sorry." Olivia exhaled, wanting to console this *child* stood in front of her, because essentially, that was what he was and what he had been when it happened. She could see the burden of that secret etched into his tense shoulders, his drooping posture. "Do you think Emma would be comfortable coming in and giving a statement?" Harry dropped his hand to look at the detectives at that comment, quickly shaking his head.

"Please—she can't know that I told you." His voice was panicked. "She's been trying to put it behind her, forget what he did."

Olivia sighed.

"I can't promise that we won't talk to her, but I can promise you that if we do, she won't know it came from you. Maybe we found a diary entry or something. Is that enough of a compromise, Harry?" she enquired.

Harry stood silently, indecision painted across his face.

"How old is Emma?" Lawrence piped up, glancing between them.

"She's my twin," Harry blurted out. "We'll be out of Newquay soon, and on to bigger and better things." A smile crept across his face as he talked about putting his hometown behind him.

Not our girl, Lawrence seemed to say with his fresh glance to Olivia. She nodded. Seventeen was certainly too old for Fisher's affair, and it seemed like Emma had gotten away from him fairly quickly. If Lydia's story was to be believed, Fisher's victim had been seeing him for some time—not a singular attempt at his flat.

"And when did this incident occur?" Lawrence asked.

"About a year ago. No—a year and a half ago, actually," Harry replied, continuing to fidget against the wall.

"Thank you for speaking with us, Mr. Price. I know that wasn't easy." Olivia began to wrap up the meeting. "Is there anything else that you'd like to tell us about Mr. Fisher?"

Harry glanced over to the wall of empty computers before turning back to them.

"Only that I hope the prick rots in hell," he spat out, emboldened as he spoke of his disdain. His features were clearly etched in anger.

Olivia wasn't sure it was enough to incite deadly violence against the English teacher, though, but she made a mental note of it, nonetheless.

"Understood. You may return to class, Mr. Price." The blonde-haired boy bolted out of the room before Olivia had the chance to finish saying his name.

"Well then," Lawrence sighed, looking over to Olivia. "That was interesting."

"Agreed," she responded. "There definitely was an escalation from Emma's instance to whoever his 15-year-old victim's experience ended up being."

"Plus, the fact that nearly two years ago, he'd already been so emboldened as to invite a student over to his flat?" Lawrence let out a heavy sigh. "That complicates things, don't you think? It might mess with our timeline."

Olivia didn't have the opportunity to respond before the brunette who had stormed off earlier sullenly marched into the room. Principal Hargraves peered in from the hallway, silently gesturing that it was, in fact, the girl that Olivia had brought up previously.

"She's requested to speak to you both alone..." he added, glancing at Bev.

"Um..." Liv looked at the trained appropriate adult, who jumped up realising it was her they were talking about. "I mean, would that be okay?"

Bev turned to the teen and gave her an encouraging smile.

"I'm here to make sure everything goes as it should," she explained. "Everything you say here is confidential, of course."

The girl shook her head.

"Would you prefer me to wait outside?" Bev pressed. "I can do that."

The teen nodded slowly, and the AA pulled her bag over her shoulder and picked up her folder.

"I'll be in the corridor if you need me," she whispered to the detectives.

Olivia gave her a reluctant thumbs up, at which point she disappeared out of the room with the headteacher. In an attempt to avoid a petulant sigh, Olivia let herself take in a deep breath and hold it for a moment.

"Hello there," Dean said first. "I'm Detective

Inspector Lawrence, this is Detective Inspector Austin. And you are?" He perked up as he spoke to the teen girl who shrunk into the chair opposite them.

"Francesca Atkinson," she muttered, slouching further.

"It's nice to meet you Francesca." Lawrence smiled. "Do you know why you're here? Was there a reason you didn't want another adult present for this conversation?"

"Dunno," she shrugged, picking at her nails.

Olivia leaned forward, interlacing her fingers with her elbows propped on her knees. *Don't pull away like that,* she wanted to scold the brunette. There was a forced distance to Francesca's body language, like she was trying to give off an aloof air when in fact she was puppeteering the whole scene.

"When we announced to the school that Mr. Fisher had passed away, you stormed off, quite upset," Olivia observed. She charted every inch of Francesca's face, looking for any sign of emotion. There was the tiniest flinch, which Francesca quickly covered with a smirk.

"It's bollocks that you had to call the whole school in." The teen sighed with a shrug. "It's not like Mr. Fisher even knew most of the kids here. You lot are wasting our time."

"Is that so?" Lawrence asked, a bit of shock on his face.

Olivia assumed it was for show; although she reminded herself again that she couldn't always be sure when it came to her partner. The lines got blurry on occasion—what was performance and what was real? Olivia wished she knew better.

Francesca's scoff brought Olivia back to the current moment.

"Did you have Mr. Fisher as a teacher?" Olivia asked patiently. She lifted and let go of her shoulders.

"Yeah," the teen replied. "And so what? A lot of people did."

"It must be upsetting to lose someone you know, even if they were a teacher," Lawrence led on, trying to pull any sort of emotion out of Francesca.

She glared at him.

"And what if I don't care?" she asked, raising her eyebrows.

Olivia chuckled a bit.

"You're really good at the tough girl façade, aren't you?" she asked, again leaning forward in her chair, asserting her space in Francesca's bubble. *I see you*, she wanted to whisper. *You're not fooling me.*

"I'm not *fazed* by a couple of detectives in shabby clothes, if that's what you mean," the girl spat back. "There are terrorists all over the place and you two coppers are in here hassling kids about *teachers* instead? There are real bad guys out there to catch." She saw the look on Olivia's face and ran with it. "I bet you guys are baby cops, aren't you? You're here to help us 'grieve' but never had to do it yourself."

Liv sighed; she could feel the conversation heading to a place she didn't want it to go.

"We're here to help," she answered firmly. "Are *you* grieving Mr Fisher's death?"

She felt the pressure of Lawrence's reassuring hand against her arm. Either that or he was warning her, but she was fine.

"Touched a nerve?" observant Francesca noticed, eyes on Dean's comforting touch. "Interesting. So, you *have* done some grieving, huh? Cried when your dog died? Hamster maybe? Fish? Husband? Yes. Maybe he wanted to die just to get *away* from you!"

Olivia raised her hands in mock defence.

"You know what? How about instead of continually avoiding the damn questions, you just tell us what you know about Mr. Fisher? Stop hiding behind that fucking smirk!" She slammed her fist down on the table. Her vision was tinged red, her lungs suddenly out of breath. *That little bitch!*

"Olivia," Lawrence warned. His hand was wrapped around her bicep, pulling her back into her chair. She hadn't even noticed that she'd propelled herself halfway out of the seat in an attempt to get into Francesca's face. She felt her heart racing and ran a shaky hand over her face. It wasn't the student's business to know that actually, yes, she'd seen grief first-hand, the most horrifying type anyone could ever dream of. And coupling what the girl had said along with the mood her nightmare had left her in—and the fact it was that time of the month—

she should have known better to hold herself back more.

"I'm-I'm sorry," Olivia apologised, shaking her head as she slowly sunk back into her chair, face aghast. "Something came over me, and it's no excuse, but..."

"You *should* be sorry," Francesca shot back without letting her finish, anger flaring in her own eyes. "Aren't you supposed to be *helping* students who are having a hard time right now?" she demanded. "We're *grieving* here."

It was at that moment that Olivia saw the tears in the teenager's eyes and noted the way her voice caught in her throat when she'd said the last part.

Before Liv could attempt to placate her more and apologise again, the girl stood up and stormed off toward the door.

"Francesca!" Lawrence called. "Wait!" He got up and started to follow her out of the room.

"Please don't," she called over her shoulder before breaking into a sprint down the hallway.

Silence swarmed the detective pair, both sets of eyes glued to the open door and fast-disappearing image of the brunette student bolting down the hall.

Mr Hargraves and the AA poked their head out of a room further down and turned to watch the last of Francesca's figure before she disappeared out of the fire exit.

"What the hell was that?" Lawrence asked, turning to face Olivia.

"I—I don't know," she stammered. "I saw red. She said... I mean, today has been..." she stood up. "I think I just need some fresh air."

"Clearly," Lawrence huffed. "That girl is obviously traumatised, Liv! I honestly believe she could be Fisher's *one*! You can't be going into a full rage in her face, for God's sake! I know you're going through..."

"I'm sorry," Olivia muttered, stopping him before he said what she knew he was going to. She'd done exactly what she'd vowed she wouldn't. *Don't let your past interact with your present.* She'd tried so hard to keep them apart. To keep everything separate and do her job. Now, the way Lawrence was looking at her made her want to disappear. "I'm going to grab some air. I'll be back in five."

She rushed down the same hall that Francesca had fled down and past a confused Bev on her way from the room, shoes ringing against the floor.

Before she knew it, she was back outside.

Fuck.

12

"What the hell?" she asked herself, trying not to shake slightly. It had all happened so quickly; one moment she was calm and meeting a potential victim, the next, she was yelling in a teenager's face.

"Get a grip," Olivia muttered, lifting her face to the sky. What was it about that girl that had hit such a raw nerve for her? And whatever the hell that nerve was, she shouldn't have let it turn into an outburst. She was a 35-year-old woman, after all, not some hormonal teen.

Francesca had reminded her of someone, though. That had to be part of it. The caginess, the caustic banter, the inability to answer a question straight. It felt a little too familiar.

The realisation hit her like a slap to the face.

Me.

Francesca had reminded Olivia of herself—in the

weeks after the Oxford Street attack, when everyone wanted answers and all she wanted was to escape from the noise of everything. Not to mention the guilt she had felt. It was like a cacophonous band had taken up residence in Olivia's head and wouldn't let her sleep or think or have a normal conversation. Everything was ten times more difficult than it had to be, and because of that, Olivia had become irritable and avoidant.

"Fuck," she exhaled again. *I've just yelled at an already-traumatised child.* Francesca was holding secrets, but the answer wasn't to blow up in her face about it—hell, that was about the worst thing she could have done.

Calm down, she scolded herself. *Breathe.* She allowed her eyes to close as she focused on the air coming in through her nose and into her lungs before releasing out her mouth. In. Out.

By the time she had let her eyes welcome the world back into her sight, Lawrence had made it back outside. He had his coat on and hers, coupled with her bag, on his arm.

"I'm so sorry." She exhaled, searching her partner's face. He wouldn't look at her.

"I've told the officers to take over. We're leaving for the day." Lawrence's face was stoic, unreadable.

Olivia tried to step into his line of sight, but to no avail.

"Wait—Lawrence. Lawrence, please just look at me," Olivia almost pleaded, following behind him almost like a lost puppy. "It won't happen again. And I mean it.

It *won't!*" Her partner continued to stalk towards the car.

"Get in," he growled with the shake of his head. "We're going to go for a drive and cool off, and *then* we'll decide if we can go back to the station or if *you* need to be done for the day."

A protest died in Olivia's throat before it could even make its way to her mouth. What was she supposed to say to that?

He opened the door for her.

"Please, Liv. Just get in the car." He sounded tired, Olivia realised. Was it really so difficult working with her? She thought that she'd managed to overcome the reputation of being the pitied, traumatised co-worker. So much progress lost in the space of a five second outburst. How could she do that?

She gave Lawrence another look, but he simply stared straight ahead.

Without a word, Olivia ducked her head to settle into the car. A moment later, Lawrence joined. They sat in silence as he started the engine and drove out of the school's car park.

"I'm really sorry," Olivia spoke through gritted teeth. Tears welled to her eyes, but she refused to let them fall.

"I know," he replied, releasing his walls slightly. "That still wasn't okay, though. And after we'd dismissed her AA? The shit we'll get into if the girl makes a complaint?"

"You're right," Olivia agreed, ready to open up. "I'm

sorry. I'll take the full blame for it, and I understand why it happened. Stress from a bad dream meant my head wasn't in the right place this morning, and then what she said about terrorists and grief and my husband wanting to die to get away from me... I just... It won't happen again. You have my word."

Lawrence sat listening to everything she said, eyes firmly on the road.

Olivia felt weak at the depths of her thoughts she'd just relayed to him, but it was necessary. He had to know.

"Thanks for pulling me back," she whispered, gaze downcast towards her palm.

He nodded wordlessly.

"Okay," she sighed after another moment of stillness. He was annoyed with her, and he had every right. "Hopefully, Francesca will want to speak to us again once she's calmed down. Did you manage to get the name of the other girl before I ruined everything?"

There was another pause and Lawrence took a deep breath.

"Before I left, Principal Hargraves said her name is Mia Baker," he explained, eyes glued to the road. "She talked with some of the grief counsellors today and agreed that she'll call us tomorrow."

"That's good," Olivia sighed against the tension. "We also need to check in with Lydia Fisher's alibi. Her sister was the one she was staying with, right?"

Lawrence nodded tersely.

"Look, Dean. I said I'm sorry. Do you want to keep sulking about it, or do you want to yell at me, or do you want to do something else?" Olivia demanded, throwing her hands up in the air. "If you need to shout, then do it! This... this limbo you have me in is excruciating!"

After her mini outburst, the car fell silent apart from the low sounds of BBC radio one in the background.

"I just... I need a bit of time. Just like you needed some air," Lawrence whispered. Dread filled Olivia's chest. The thought of disappointing Lawrence practically broke her. She could handle yelling or screaming. But defeat? Because of her? She didn't know how much she could bear it.

"Understood," she replied, tight lipped. "Well, if you want, you can drop me off at the station and then go for a drive or something. I'm happy to keep working on the case until you're ready to...ready to work with me again." Her words grated against her head; *how could you be so stupid?* she wanted to scream at herself.

"That sounds like a good idea," Lawrence agreed, turning the radio up, signalling the end of their conversation.

"Great," Olivia mumbled, staring outside her window to hide the welling of fresh tears. *You manage to fuck up everything good, don't you?*

THEY SPENT the rest of the drive in silence apart from pitiful tunes on the radio, Olivia kneading her hands together while Lawrence tightly gripped the steering wheel.

"And Liv?" he called out as she began to exit the car once they were back at Newquay Police Station. It was the first thing he'd said since he had agreed to drop her off.

She looked back at him, properly making eye contact.

"Don't call me," he said firmly. "I'll let you know when I'm ready."

Olivia's jaw opened slightly, the words stinging more than any others had during the past year. Pursing her lips together, she slammed the car door shut and quickly turned to face the station before Lawrence could see her crestfallen face. The crackle of loose pebbles under tires signalled to Olivia that he was driving away.

You deserved that, her inner narrator crooned at her. *Poor, damaged Olivia. Can't even bother to interview a victim decently.* She let out something between a strangled scream and a cry. It was brief, but it released the anguish she had felt building up since Lawrence had stormed out of the school after her.

Wiping away the start of her tears, Olivia straightened herself out quickly. She turned to face the entrance to the station.

You've got this, Liv, she assured herself. Why did she feel like she'd just cost herself a precious friendship, then?

13

"Yes, I'm calling to speak with a Margaret Anderson—is she available?" Olivia spoke dejectedly into the phone, trying not to stare at Lawrence's empty desk. Lydia's sister still had the maiden name Anderson, something Olivia had made note of before calling. She offhandedly pressed 'record' on the machine just in case Lawrence wanted to listen in after he got back from his drive.

"I'm Margaret Anderson," the caller responded.

"Brilliant. Miss Anderson, my name is Olivia Austin; I'm with the Devon and Cornwall Police."

The woman cleared her throat.

"Oh yes; Lydia said you'd be calling," Margaret responded. "And please, Margaret is fine."

"All right, well Margaret, I know you've heard by now that your sister's husband, Simon Fisher, has passed away. You should know that this call is being recorded, by the way," Olivia added.

"That's quite okay, I've got nothing to hide," she answered. "And yes, I heard the bastard had a meetup with the ground from his flat yesterday morning."

Olivia was a little shocked by the rage in her voice.

"You didn't like him, then?" Olivia asked, pressing further.

"Well, Lydia felt the need to leave, didn't she? That's enough of a reason for me," Margaret replied with a hint of sarcasm.

"That's fair. Did you know Simon well?" Olivia enquired. She knew that the main purpose of this call was to get verification of Lydia's alibi, but it felt like too good of an opportunity to give up.

"Not terribly, no," Margaret answered cautiously. "Back when he and Lydia were still together, they'd have me over for supper every now and again. He was fine up until he wasn't, in my book."

Her voice had a certain caustic quality about it; Olivia found it oddly comforting. At least she wasn't the only one with a bitter attitude towards the world.

"I see," Olivia mused, biting her bottom lip. "And do you know why your sister left Mr. Fisher?"

Margaret scoffed on the other end.

"Lydia's about as closed off as they come," she replied. "When she showed up to my doorstep, a sobbing mess, I was just grateful she'd come to me and not run off to who knows where. So no, I didn't ask, and

Lydia didn't bother telling me. All I know is that you've got to be some sick bastard for someone as loyal as my sister to leave your sorry arse."

The vitriol in Margaret's voice was evident; she truly cared that her sister had been wronged.

"I understand, Miss Anderson," Olivia replied calmly.

"Do you though? Margaret asked. "Do you have a sister, detective?"

It caught Olivia slightly off guard. She wasn't expecting to be interviewed in kind.

"I do," Olivia replied after a moment. Images of Mills' pink hair and wide smile flashed behind her eyes. Camilla was the epitome of a free spirit; how had it been that she was the one settled down with a child and husband while Olivia lived like a spinster in her cottage? She supposed it was foolish to ponder such questions. Life, after all, always had a funny way of happening.

"Do you love her to death, detective?" Margaret's tone had become grave, interrupting her thoughts.

"Well, yes. Of course I do." It was the only response Olivia could give.

"Then you'll understand that when Lydia came to me, I made sure not to ask questions," she answered. "That her safety and well-being was far greater than my curiosity."

"I understand that," Olivia agreed, mindlessly thumbing through the papers on her desk. "She's lucky to have a sister that cares so much. And, Miss Anderson,

I hope you don't mind if I ask you about the night in question."

Margaret grumbled in agreement.

"Was Lydia at your house on Saturday night?" Olivia asked.

"She was," the woman affirmed.

"And do you remember about what time she went to bed?" Olivia pressed on, jotting down *positive alibi from sister* on her notepad. After Margaret's statement, she wasn't sure that it could be counted as a rock-solid alibi, unfortunately. She seemed like the kind of person who would be willing to lie if it meant protecting her sister.

"Oh, it would have been around nine. I think we watched a movie on the telly beforehand," she answered. "Although I can't remember if that was Friday or Saturday, the more that I think about it. She falls asleep fairly quickly and sleeps like a rock."

"Understood," Olivia acknowledged. "And what time did you go to sleep?"

Margaret paused to jog her memory.

"After Lydia goes to bed, I usually clean up the kitchen and read a book until I fall asleep," she explained. "It must have been around 11 p.m. That's about when I get tired enough for it to be worth it to turn in."

Olivia made sure to write everything down.

"Great. And the next morning—what happened then?" She tried to make her deeper enquiry sound as light as she could.

"Well," Margaret answered. "I woke up around 7 in the morning. Brewed a pot, turned on the local radio, and sat down to listen as I sipped. It's a nice ritual of mine. Then, a friend who lives in that area sent me a text and mentioned something about a police scene at Lydia's flat. Rumours of a dead body and all that. I wasn't going to just ignore it, so I woke up Lydia as quickly as possible at that point." The woman's voice quickened as she described the events of Sunday morning. "It all happened so fast, Lydia practically left in her nightgown. She forgot her phone, so I stayed home and twiddled my thumbs until she returned. And that was when—"

Margaret stopped herself from continuing the story. There was silence on the other end of the phone. Was she crying? Or, carefully orchestrating what she was going to say next?

"That..." she continued slowly, "was when Lydia told me what I had suspected. Simon... well, he was *dead*."

She let out a long breath.

Olivia noted the pause. Anything could mean everything.

"And that was all that was said to you?" she asked, pressing on. "Nothing else? No matter how insignificant you think it is."

Margaret cleared her throat.

"Only that she'd spoken with police at the scene and that they wanted to call and confirm her alibi," she offered. "And trust me, detective. Lydia takes sleeping pills at night—prescribed and everything. She wouldn't have been able to wake up in the middle of the night, let alone drive herself across town. You can ask her doctor, too. They're prescription."

Her reiteration of that fact was noted too. *Trying too hard to protect her sister? Possibly.*

Olivia tapped her pen on her chin, wishing that Lawrence had been with her to give his input. She could almost picture his expression on hearing that part.

"That was very helpful, Miss Anderson," she assured her. "We'll be sure to follow up with all loose ends. Is there anything else you'd like us to know while the investigation is open? Any enemies you know of that Mr. Fisher may have had? Arguments? Fallouts? Bad blood?"

Margaret sighed, the tone of it suggesting she was on the verge of irritation.

"Like I said before, I didn't know the man that well," she answered. "I should have known he was up to no good and warned Lydia before he broke her heart, but I was too cautious."

Olivia picked up on her offhand comment.

"Why do you say you should have known better?" she pressed.

"Sometimes you just know that someone isn't quite right in the head." Margaret's response was firm. "That's how I felt about Simon. I didn't have anything that would prove it, though, so I just let it be. I thought that Lydia's happiness was more important than any silly gut feeling I may have had. Turns out I was wrong." She sighed, exasperated.

Olivia wrote Lydia's name down on her piece of paper with a large question mark next to it.

"Fair enough," she replied looking down at the letters of the woman's name. There was something more to this story than the women were letting on. She could feel it. "Well, that's all I need for now, Margaret." She decided against letting her suspicions be known. "Your sister has our number; please don't hesitate to reach out if you think of anything else. Thank you for your time."

"No, thank *you* for calling, Detective," Margaret replied.

The two women quickly gave their goodbyes before hanging up. Almost without thinking, Olivia pressed the button to end the recording before gazing off at the cork board Lawrence had been fussing with the day before.

The conversation had distracted her—albeit only momentarily—from the reality of her afternoon. Now that she was alone with her thoughts, the absence of her partner at his desk hit her like a brick wall.

I fucked up, she thought to herself as she stared at his empty chair. She opened her phone, ready to call him, apologise again and update him on Margaret Anderson's interview.

Don't call me. Lawrence's words rang in Olivia's ears, giving her pause.

She put her phone down onto her desk, letting out

an involuntary groan as she made peace with the fact that she shouldn't call him—at least not yet.

It's late, she reminded herself. *You're done for the day. Just write a note in case Dean comes in and get ready for another start tomorrow.*

With a dejected sigh, Olivia started to pack up her things. Only once she was completely ready to leave and certain Lawrence wasn't about to push through the doors to their office with a grin on his face and a gentle and forgiving lecture did she settle down to write her note to her partner.

She hesitated for several moments, pen hovering above notepad. Where to even begin? With the shake of her head, she finally pressed the end of the cheap biro into the fresh paper.

SPOKE WITH MARGARET ANDERSON. *Cleared sister Lydia but also seems ready to lie for her. Recording on computer. Text/call with any questions.*

SHE STARED AT THE NOTE. Was that enough? Too much? Olivia huffed as she debated her inscription for her partner.

SORRY AGAIN. -Liv.

THE WORDS SPILLED from the pen before she had the opportunity to second guess them. Afterwards, she rushed from the police station, feeling as if she herself was fleeing a crime scene.

Was it fair of her to leave the note? Was the note something Lawrence needed? The clear evening air in the car park did little to assuage the sinking feeling in her chest. It was as though the asphalt was beckoning to her, inviting her to curl up inside of it.

You'll be okay, she told herself. *Lawrence will talk to you soon.* Still, her phone burned in her pocket, another reminder that she couldn't call her partner and confidante.

She hurried herself into the waiting Uber before she could worry about it too much. After all, she still had a case to solve.

He'll call soon, she assured herself as the car took off into the cold, empty night.

14

Morning came and went without sign of Detective Inspector Lawrence at the station, try as Olivia might to will his presence through the doorway. About an hour into the stack of paperwork that Olivia was sifting through, Det. Supt. Collins swung by to inform her that Dean had called in sick.

"He said he's hoping to be in this afternoon or tomorrow, it's hard to tell."

"Those were his exact words?" Olivia had asked, feeling the sinking feeling spread across her stomach. She couldn't tell if the disappointment was with him or herself.

"Essentially," Collins had responded before turning to leave the office. "How's the case going?" he asked, almost offhandedly.

Olivia knew her boss better than to think that he was ambivalent about her answer. She cleared her throat.

"We don't have any major suspects yet," she answered. "But we're honing in on a couple of leads. Going to the school yesterday was very helpful," she explained, twirling her pen between her fingers to avoid eye contact. Just in case her eyes gave away the secret to her terrible behaviour the day before. She glanced at Collins as she spoke her last sentence though, his broad frame filling up the doorway. "We're going to catch whoever did this. I can feel it."

He gave her a firm nod.

"Carry on," was her boss's only response before turning to exit the office with a final thumbs up. She smiled at that. It was maybe the closest she had gotten to a stamp of approval from the Superintendent. It felt good to be on the right track—although the guilt of fighting with Lawrence the day before stopped her from fully appreciating the moment. It wasn't her victory to celebrate. It was *theirs*, as a team.

Please come back soon, Lawrence, she wished as she looked back to his desk and his immaculate notes on the board right behind it. *I could really use your help.*

According to the school's records, Mr. Fisher had 67 female students currently being taught by him. It was a fairly big group to try and sift through in order to find his victim—especially if they wanted to be quiet about it.

If his paramour found out that they were looking for her, she could run for the hills. It wouldn't be fair to just start grabbing the students and asking them point blank if they had slept with their teacher, either. That would be downright cruel.

Olivia made sure to note that both Francesca Atkinson and Mia Baker were in Mr. Fisher's classes. There were also two female students who hadn't been at school that day who showed up on his rosters: Rene Farrow and Ivy Thompson. She circled those names as well. They were all important leads—that much was certain.

A thought occurred to her as she sorted through the names. It started quietly, like a whisper just below the surface of her consciousness, but soon it wouldn't stop nagging her.

She quickly dialled Lydia Fisher's number, pushing various papers aside to make space for her notepad.

"C'mon," she muttered, urging the woman to pick up.

Just when she thought Lydia wouldn't answer, she heard a click and a familiar "Hello?" echo from the other end.

"Hi, Lydia? This is DI Austin," Olivia spoke quickly, somehow nervous that Simon's wife was going to hang up on her. She leaned forward in her seat, on the edge of anticipation.

"Oh, yes. Hello, Detective," she responded quietly.

Olivia could barely hear her.

"I'm sorry, did your husband ever specify the gender of his victim?" she asked, urgency coating her voice.

Lydia hesitated.

"What? Oh," she replied. She sounded groggy—maybe even intoxicated. "I can't...I can't remember for certain but I'm nearly positive he said 'she.' What are you insinuating, detective?"

Olivia bit the corner of her lip in contemplation.

"Apologies for being so blunt, Lydia," she answered. "I had to confirm with you if we knew the gender of his victim before we eliminated half of the student population. Doing less than that would have been negligent. You're certain he would have slept with a girl?"

Olivia felt cruel as the words escaped her lips, but she knew it needed to be asked.

Lydia seemed flustered.

"I...I understand, detective," she fumbled. "Forgive me, the question just caught me off guard. Yes, it was a woman—girl. I would have known if—" She cut herself off.

"Of course, you would have known," Olivia reassured Simon's wife before the woman spiralled again. "I just needed to double check. Thank you for taking the time to answer."

"Of course, detective. Is there anything else that I can help you with?" Lydia asked.

"Only if there's anything else you've thought of since we last chatted," Olivia replied, trying to be gentle after her rather harsh words earlier. It wasn't every day she asked a newly widowed woman if her husband had in fact been sleeping with a fifteen-year-old boy instead of a girl.

"Not that I can think of, to be completely honest," Lydia answered. "Apologies, I've just woken up from a nap, so my head isn't all quite here at the moment. I heard that you talked with Margaret yesterday," she observed.

"I did indeed," Olivia commented. "She spoke highly of you and confirmed your alibi."

"Oh, that's good to hear," Lydia sighed. *A little too relieved perhaps?* "Have you figured out who his student was?"

Olivia watched as Tim entered their small office and gave her a little wave before he sat down.

"Not yet, Lydia," she answered and then paused. She knew this wasn't going to be easy to hear. "You know that even once we do, privacy laws mean that we can't tell you who it was." She winced as she spoke the truth aloud.

The other end of the phone remained silent.

"I understand," Lydia choked out eventually. "And that's good. It really is. You should be protecting her."

Her sentences were choppy; Olivia could tell she was holding back tears.

"You'll be okay, though?" she asked the woman. "You've been given the numbers for the bereavement counsellors?"

"I have, thank you," Lydia sighed. "It's just a lot, Detective." She sniffed and cleared her throat. "If that's all..."

"Oh right," Olivia exhaled. "It is, yes. I'll let you get back to...your nap. Don't forget you have our number if anything comes up."

"Of course," she replied. "Thank you for calling, detective."

Liv heard the sound of a hushed voice in the background.

"Thank you for being so forthright, Lydia," she said, choosing to ignore that it might have been Margaret telling her what to say to sound innocent. "You've been an immense help."

She let the words hang in the air for a moment before hanging up then sighed as she placed her phone on the desk.

She wanted to believe Lydia, but she also knew how unreliable witness statements could be—especially when loved ones were involved. Even if Lydia was positive that Simon had been sleeping with a girl, she could have filled in that detail herself—or Simon could have lied.

If only Lawrence was here, she thought to herself. *I'd be able to bounce ideas off him, get new perspectives. I hope he comes back soon.*

A now-familiar ache blossomed in her chest as she thought about the absence of her partner. He had such a strong perspective on the world, and on other people. A keen acuity about him.

Olivia was worried she'd started getting too tangled in the case to have an understanding of the full picture. She looked at the corkboard on the side, trying to connect the dots. Someone out there hated Simon Fisher enough to enter his flat and kill him.

Deciding it was Lydia seemed too easy. Francesca maybe? If she was in fact his victim, would she have wanted him dead? Maybe she felt scorned that he'd tried to end things with her. Her attitude definitely left a lot to be desired, but was she a killer? No, who knew? Maybe her parents had found out? An angry dad? Big enough to throw a fighting man over a balcony?

Her thoughts were interrupted by a call coming in from the medical examiner's office. A flutter of excitement rose up Olivia's throat. It wasn't Lawrence, but at least whoever was calling was good company. Plus, it would be another distraction at that.

"Hello, Detective Inspector Austin speaking," she answered the phone, glancing around to see if Tim was paying attention. He picked up his mug as though on cue and made his way out the door.

She could see through the internal window that a couple of other detectives had their heads down at their desks, but no one seemed interested in her conversation.

"Detective Austin, hello," a familiar voice greeted her, sending a renewed flutter deep through Olivia's chest. His voice was so smooth, like chocolate fondue or a good shot of whiskey.

"Dr. James," she exhaled. Whatever he was calling about, it was certainly work-related. She was in a professional setting for goodness' sake, not a country club.

"Indeed." He laughed lightly. "It's good to hear your voice, Detective, I can't lie."

That sent a blush straight to Olivia's cheeks. *Calm down,* she scolded herself. *This is your co-worker, don't do this again.*

"Likewise," she managed to get out, her mouth suddenly much drier than it had been a couple of minutes prior. She reached for a glass of water.

"Well," Dr. James sighed with a clearing of his throat, breaking the silence Olivia hadn't even noticed had crept around them.

"Sorry," she blurted out. "I got distracted. I'm assuming something's come up in the Fisher case?"

"Your assumption would be correct," Elliott agreed. "We finished the autopsy this morning. We're officially declaring it a murder. He was beaten brutally, and it seems like with objects as well as with fists."

"Harsh overkill," Olivia exhaled.

The medical examiner hummed in agreement.

"My best guess is it was some sort of pipe or cylindrical object," he informed her. "Probably metal, from the intensity of the impact, although I wouldn't completely rule out a sturdy piece of wood, depending on the strength of the killer."

Olivia jotted down every piece of information that Dr. James explained to her.

"Are you able to tell if he was dead before the fall?" Olivia asked, wincing a bit as she thought about those dreadful moments before impact. *Maybe he was spared that.*

"Inconclusive results on that, unfortunately, but based on bruising and trajectory angles, I'd wager it's more likely than not that the fall is what ultimately killed him. It was probably a push, but again, hard to say with factors such as the wind and whether or not he could have stumbled off the ledge."

Olivia sighed, willing the images of a crushed Mr. Fisher to stay out of her dreams. She'd had enough nightmares recently to last a lifetime.

"Anything else of note from the autopsy?" she asked, looking through her notes.

"A couple of things, actually," Dr. Elliot responded. "He had some alcohol in his system, as well as an anti-anxiety medication. And this is what really gets me. Whoever the killer was, they were incredibly careful to avoid leaving any DNA on Mr. Fisher's body. Usually, something as violent as this results in tissue, blood, or fingerprints being left from the assailant. Often the victim is able to get some sort of DNA on them in the struggle."

Interesting.

"The crime scene analysts thought that the killer may

have worn gloves," Olivia observed, doing her best to understand what the implications of a clean killer meant. "Normally, this kind of overkill isn't premeditated or organised. It's usually fuelled by passion and therefore more likely to be sloppy. But clearly whoever killed him took precautions."

"That's what I was thinking, too," Dr. James agreed. "We were able to find one thing: a long blonde hair stuck in one of the lacerations on his back. It didn't have any tissue from the root of the hair, and it could have just been from around the apartment or outside. Still, I thought I should mention it."

Olivia wrote that down and circled it. The hair could have come from anywhere, but it seemed unlikely for a random strand floating in the wind to stick itself into one of his cuts.

Doubly interesting.

"That's great, Elliot," she replied, excitement rising in her voice. "It's not incriminating, but it could help us narrow down suspects."

"You finally called me Elliot." The doctor chuckled.

Olivia's cheeks turned a bright crimson once again. Thankfully, he couldn't see her.

"Sorry, Dr. James," Olivia clarified with a nervous laugh.

"No. I like it. Please, it's Elliot," he insisted, more warmth in his voice than was fair considering how sweet he already sounded.

"Okay, *Elliot*," Olivia replied, a smile slowly unfurling across her face.

"That's better." He laughed. "Anyway, yes. The hair isn't necessarily from the killer, but it could be helpful in the investigation."

"Brilliant," Olivia replied, the smile still glued on her face. Something about speaking with the doctor just made her feel positively calm, as though she were floating in the clouds, not tethered to the ground in cold Cornwall.

"That's all I have so far," Dr. James sighed.

I wish you had more to tell me, Olivia thought to herself, though she didn't dare say it aloud. Especially not in the middle of the office. *If only Mills and mum could see me now.*

"Right, well, that's been very helpful, *Elliot*." She made sure to emphasise his first name. A peal of laughter echoed from the phone.

"It sounds so good coming from you," he replied, voice also somewhat calm.

Is he flirting with me? The thought jolted Olivia a bit, as though she'd just splashed her face with cold water.

There was no denying, he was good-looking, and it wasn't as though she was an ogre herself, but the thought of someone flirting with *her*, Olivia Austin, eternal fuck-up and damaged goods of a woman…

She realised she hadn't considered that someone could ever be attracted to her again. At least, not anyone that she viewed any kind of longevity with. Three-night stands and pity sex didn't count. But someone who actually knew her and had at least an idea of her past? How could anyone want to be associated with her after knowing *that*?

Then again, she could obviously be reading into it too much. It was easy to infer with Dr. James; he had such an openness to him, she could easily create connections that weren't necessarily there. After all, a man like that had to be attached to *someone*.

"It's a nice name," she replied, quieting her internal conflict in order to respond to the medical examiner.

"I'm glad you think so, Detective Austin."

"Please, if I'm to call you Elliot, you should call me Olivia." She smiled. In her mind's eye, she could see him looking at her. Mischievous yet earnest eyes, full of depth in all of their green glory. *Call me Olivia.*

"Well then, Olivia," Elliot replied, voice full again of that earnestness that almost broke Olivia's heart every time she heard it. "It was a pleasure to speak to you."

"Likewise. You've been extremely helpful with the case," Olivia replied demurely, reminding herself that she was still inside a police station, not at home with a glass of wine. The casual nature of their conversation made it feel like she could almost fool herself into thinking they were sharing a candlelit dinner.

"Always happy to help," Elliot agreed. "Well, I better be off. I'll call if anything else comes up."

"Brilliant," Olivia murmured, the smile now dancing on and off her face.

"Brilliant," the doctor agreed. "Until next time, Olivia."

"Until next time, Elliot."

15

The line stayed open for a moment before the telling click at the end of the call came through. Olivia stared at her desk without really seeing anything at all. *Had that really just happened?* she wondered.

In some ways, she felt guilty. And even hearing herself think it, she knew it sounded daft, but she couldn't help but feel bad for enjoying the light-hearted conversation with the doctor.

Of course, she knew Rhys wouldn't want her to spend the rest of her life moping around pining for him and what could have been. Her mother constantly said as much. But a proper relationship? Proper feelings? A year and a half later?

She left the confines of her office, hoping that a change of scenery to the kitchen for cup of something might force her to stop this train of thought.

Don't get ahead of yourself.

She poured herself some coffee from Tim's infamous cafetiere, but a firm tap on her shoulder almost made her drop it.

She spun around, half expecting to see Lawrence standing there with a disgruntled but acquiescing face. Instead, the goofy grin of one Police Constable Andrew Shaw greeted her. She let out a surprised gasp.

"Shaw?" She was reminded how surprisingly good the officer looked in his uniform. His hair, quite in contrast to Sunday morning's bed head, was immaculately styled, and there was no trace of an afternoon shadow on his chin. He could have been the poster boy for the police force.

She tried not to think about the fact that she'd seen Shaw in his 'altogether' and that his body was just as impressive as the way he cleaned up.

"Olivia," he replied with a smirk. She wanted to smack him for startling her, yet somehow, it was also somewhat of a relief to see him. He had a calming presence about him.

"What are you doing in the office?" she managed to ask, eyes still wide with surprise. She leaned against the counter, attempting nonchalance.

"I had to run a few things up to Grumps and Susan," he answered. "And then I saw you sneaking out of your office. I couldn't leave without saying hello. Plus, I wanted to make sure that you got home okay after…

Well, after everything on Sunday morning." Amusement flashed behind Shaw's eyes.

Olivia flushed. *Of course, he's bringing Sunday up.*

"That was quite the adventure, wasn't it?" she commented, holding the warm mug of coffee in her hands.

"You can say that again." Shaw laughed. "I started the night as one of the most eligible bachelors in the whole of Devon and Cornwall Police and finished the next morning with a lovely detective fleeing my flat."

His eyebrows danced as he spoke, his voice tickled with amusement.

"Um, sorry to break it to you, but you're *still* an eligible bachelor," Olivia teased, challenging him with her stare. "And sorry about my attitude when I woke up. I'm a misery in the mornings."

Shaw rolled his eyes with mock bother.

"I could've told you that," he retorted. He had placed his hand on the counter a mere foot from Olivia's hip. When had that happened? The two stood in a tense quiet, neither daring to look away from the other. *What's your move, Shaw?* Olivia asked herself.

Ever since he'd turned up at Sam Mercers house and essentially 'saved the day', she'd felt a bond with him. Some kind of connection. Whether it was because she most probably owed him her life, or there was something deeper there. But the fact that she'd left Susan's party with the intention of having sex with him meant something at least.

"So, where's Dean?" Shaw asked, breaking the silence.

Olivia's eyebrows rose. Did her colleagues assume it was weird to see her without her partner nearby?

"Oh," she started, debating if it was worth scrambling for an excuse or best to just tell Shaw the truth. *My partner can't stand to be in my company because I screamed in the face of an abused child.* It had a nice ring to it.

Andrew tilted his head, waiting for her response, still maintaining close eye contact.

"He was, um," the staff kitchen lights suddenly felt a little too bright. "He called in sick this morning, so I'm in by myself." She hoped Shaw didn't detect the forlornness in her voice.

A gentle laugh from him made her release her breath, realising he wasn't as good at reading her body language as Lawrence was. *Of course, he isn't good at reading your body language*, she reprimanded herself. *You've spent all of three waking hours in the same room as him.*

"That's unfortunate," he replied with a devilish gleam in his eye. "Not like him to be off sick. You two make a good pair, by the way."

She let his comment linger in the air for a moment.

He diverted his cheeky stare down to her lips and then back up to her eyes.

"I'm not sure what you're insinuating, Andrew," she replied, keeping her voice low so as not to get the attention of the office gossips. "Professionally, absolutely. We're a great team."

He was almost towering over her at this point, and she had to tilt her chin up a bit in order to meet his flirty gaze with her steady one.

"Of course," he agreed, his voice matching her own tone. "An impressive professional record, I've been told."

His radio crackled, and he took a deep breath, shook his head, and moved back out of her personal space.

"Listen, I've got to get going." He sighed reluctantly. "But I wanted to give you this first." He reached out his hand to reveal a small piece of paper with his name and number scribbled down.

Olivia bit her lip to stop from smiling broadly, a singular eyebrow shooting up as if to say *are you fucking kidding me?*

"You're honestly trying to pick me up in the staff kitchen, *Duracell?*" she demanded, looking from the note to Shaw in amazement. She emphasised his nickname, which prompted a light laugh from him.

"Not trying to *pick you up*," he replied with an easy smile. "Just giving you a way to communicate in case you needed to *debrief* more about the other night."

Olivia couldn't tell if he was seriously attempting earnestness or just toying with her.

"*Debrief?*" she asked, settling in for a mini interrogation.

"*Talk,*" Shaw insisted, raising his hands in mock defence. "I just want to make sure you feel comfortable about what happened and that you know you can reach out if you need to."

She didn't quite know what to do with that information. Was Shaw actually concerned about her feelings?

He gently set the note next to Olivia on the counter, once again entering her personal space briefly before pulling back.

"And if you feel great about what happened and how Sunday went," he explained, his voice almost a whisper. "That's fine by me. I just don't want you to feel like anything's been left *unresolved.*"

Trina came into the kitchen to put her mug in the sink. She saw them both, gave a weak smile, and ducked back out quickly.

Shaw cleared his throat.

"I appreciate it," Olivia responded after a minute, making sure that no one else was loitering by the door. "Don't think that means I'll definitely call, though. But still. It's a nice thought." She glanced down at the paper but still without taking it.

"My pleasure, Detective Austin," Andrew replied with a tell-tale smirk before he gave a small bow, mostly a nod of his head. It was *almost* charming.

"Have a good shift," Olivia offered as he walked away. She looked down to the note and tapped her cup of coffee, indecision plaguing her thoughts. What would it imply if she took it? If she didn't?

"You and Duracell getting friendly?" DC Tim Harris' question brought Olivia back to reality.

He reached past her and surveyed his nearly empty cafetiere.

"Not at all," she snapped, trying her best to remain stoic. "He just..."

Both of their eyes rested on PC Shaw's note, his number sunny side up.

"Uh, apologies, Liv," Tim answered. "I didn't mean to insinuate..."

She saw almost saw him wince at the sheer awkwardness of the situation. DC Harris was absolutely harmless. It wasn't his fault, in this case, that she felt in order to get *over* something, she had to get *under* someone else. It was her own flaw. She'd seen Andrew at Susan's party and spent copious amounts of time being charmed by him before wanting to go back to his flat. She'd made her bed, and now it was time to lie in it.

She watched her colleague refill his cafetiere. Always thinking of others, he was.

"Sorry Tim," she apologised. "I didn't mean to snap at you, I'm just... I'm on edge, I guess."

"Happens to the best of us," he replied, though Olivia was certain he never made *those* kinds of mistakes. "No offense taken. I shouldn't have even asked. Biccy?"

He offered a pack of digestives toward her. Now she felt even worse. He smiled when she declined and pushed the plunger down to make the next batch of coffee for the office.

"See you in a bit." He gave her shoulder a reassuring squeeze before he left Olivia alone with her thoughts.

Fuck, she thought to herself. *How long am I going to have to deal with this gossip mill?*

With as much discretion as she could muster, Olivia quietly scooped up the paper containing Shaw's phone number. *Just in case I need to berate him for talking about me,* she assured herself as she slipped it into her pocket. She almost believed herself, too.

AFTER A LONG DAY of following rabbits down holes of leads, Olivia finally felt ready to go home. She tried her best to ignore Lawrence's empty chair as she packed up for the night. Still, it was though it was watching her every move, reminding her that she had been alone for the day. *Don't you miss him?* it seemed to taunt her.

After the day of reviewing notes and following leads, she felt thoroughly prepped for any interviews they may have to do with students or faculty in the coming days. She had pored over pages upon pages of information regarding Simon Fisher and the school he worked for. Really, all she needed to do now was get her hands on some solid evidence. She just didn't want to have to do it without Lawrence, she realised.

He'll be back in tomorrow, she told herself. *He has to be.*

After dinner and half of a glass of wine, she curled herself into her couch with Earnest and a silly rom com. She didn't particularly like the genre in and of itself, but it was the least likely to trigger a panic response, so she stuck with it in all of its saccharine glory. There was something satisfying about consuming media meant for women, too. She'd managed to get to the point where the two almost-lovers confessed their mutual, hidden feelings for one another. This one was actually quite compelling, if she allowed herself to put everything else out of her mind and focus on it.

Shaw's number burned in her pocket, reminding her that he was merely a phone call away. She pulled it out, twirling it back and forth between her fingers. Earnest batted at it, too.

"Should I call him?" she asked, turning to look at her cat. His bright yellow eyes stared back.

"You're right," she agreed, putting the now slightly crumpled piece of paper on her coffee table. "The only company I need at night is you, Mr. Earnest."

That earned her a deep meow.

"That's right," she chuckled, swirling her glass of wine before taking a sip. "It's you and me, boy."

She curled into the couch, settling in for a night alone. And although the absence of Lawrence throughout her day had made her feel slightly more lonely than normal, she realised as she sat back that she didn't mind not having anyone to share the film, a bottle of wine, or the evening with. *Getting your own space is a premium these days*, she told herself. Now all she had to do was believe that.

16

By some miracle, Olivia woke without a nightmare plaguing her dreams. Her morning routine felt light without the weight of Rhys haunting her eyes every time she closed them. She was in good spirits upon arriving to the office, and she surprised even herself with her overly positive attitude. *What's gotten into me?*

She'd barely settled into her desk and removed her coat before her mobile rang. Her caller ID identified the other end as Clara Fitzroy.

"Hello?" Olivia answered, fumbling around in her pocket to find her notepad. The analyst had a knack for calling at inopportune times.

"Olivia!" Clara exclaimed. She was excited, and just from her voice, the detective sensed it might be big. "You're not going to believe it!"

"Is that so?" Olivia asked, pressing the cap on her

pen, poised to take a flurry of notes. If Clara was good at one thing, it was rambling at the speed of a hundred words per minute. It was honestly impressive, if not sometimes frustrating to keep up with. Still, the thought of Clara's tizzy of words gave Olivia a faint smile.

"Get this..." she breathed excitedly. "I hacked Simon Fisher's computer!"

Olivia could hear the pride in her voice.

"Oh, that's brilliant!" She exclaimed. "*You're* brilliant!"

"I'm well aware of that," her colleague joked. "And I'm glad you're finally catching on, too."

Olivia could practically see her smile. It was certainly infectious.

"Buuuuuut, and it's a long but!" Clara continued. "You're going to want to hear this, Liv. He's got *hundreds* of love letters to his student on here. They're really provocative stuff. Lots of poetry and promises of love and forever."

"*Hundreds* of letters?" Olivia repeated, eyes wide. "Does it say anything about who it could be?"

There was a momentary sound of keys being pressed on the other end.

"I wish," Clara answered. "They're clearly to a dummy email account. And before you ask, it was accessed on the school's IP address, so it really could have been anyone who uses the library or IT room, if they have access. And he never uses her name; just refers to her as Bright Star. Kind of a weird nickname if you ask me."

Clara was always one for commentary; it made Olivia smile.

"Bright Star," Liv echoed. It sounded vaguely familiar, but she couldn't quite place it. "I'll call up Lawrence. He might know what that means," she started, kicking herself as the words tumbled out of her lips. *Except he doesn't want to talk to you, idiot,* she scolded herself silently.

"Great plan," Clara responded, enthusiasm thick in her voice. "I'll do some more digging later, see if there are any other indicators as to who his victim may have been or if there's anything else that would cause someone to become homicidal in his presence."

Her colleague was right. There had to be a piece to this puzzle that they were missing.

"Thank you so much, Clara," Olivia replied, already revving up her computer. "Oh, and before—"

"Already sent the love letters to your work email," the tech analyst replied before she could finish her sentence.

"Adding 'mind reader' to your list of skills," Olivia muttered with a smile. "You're going to get that drink sooner than you think if you keep up that quick analysis."

Clara laughed heartily.

"On that note, I'm off," she declared. "I'm supposed to be having a day off at the races. Talk to you later, perhaps? Good luck!"

After the call ended, Olivia stared at her phone, dread building in her stomach. She knew that despite his request, she should call Lawrence to discuss the break in the case. *Don't call me.* His words echoed in her mind, a sinister repetition that had been in the periphery of her awareness since Monday afternoon.

Her finger hovered above Lawrence's name, his smile in her phone's profile for him staring back up at her. *Just do it,* she urged herself. *The case is more important.*

Before she could press the button to ring him, their incident room-cum-office door swept open.

"Lawrence," she exhaled, looking up to see her partner walking into the office as though nothing had happened. He refused to meet her gaze.

"Detective Austin," he replied, setting his bag down at his desk.

Olivia's heart fell. He never called her by her last name. She stood frozen for a moment, unsure what to do as he quietly unpacked his things.

"Clara just called with a break in the case," she blurted out, jumping straight into their work. Their friendship might need some repairing after Monday, but it was time to solve the case, not worry about how they operated together after hours.

"She's a quick one, Clara is," he responded. "What'd she figure out?" Lawrence finally looked at Olivia. She never thought she'd be so grateful to meet the steady stare from his brown eyes. It filled her with hope. *Thank you for coming back,* she wanted to say. *I've needed you here.*

"She hacked into Mr. Fisher's computer," Olivia explained instead, returning to the case at hand. "Found loads of love letters between him and his victim."

Her emails loaded, and she clicked on the top one from Clara. Each note that was written had been attached.

"Do we know who it is?" Lawrence asked, curiosity obviously piqued. He moved over to Olivia's side to look at her screen, the scent of his cologne moving with him.

Olivia let her eyes close briefly as she welcomed in the essence of him. *I missed you.*

"No," she answered, "Only that he called her *Bright Star*. Does that mean anything to you?" She looked up at Lawrence, who hovered above her shoulder, and he looked her back, dead in the eye.

"It's Keats," he replied.

She could almost see the cogs turning behind his eyes, connections being made with every blink. She silently thanked the universe for bringing Lawrence back to her; this would have taken so much more time if she were on her own.

"The poet?" Olivia asked, studying her partner's features. She was without a doubt, impressed.

"Indeed. It's one of his most famous poems, written for his true love." He was poring over Clara's attachment of letters with Olivia as he spoke. "Their story was tragic. He died of tuberculosis after their secret engagement at the age of twenty-five. She wore his engagement ring until she herself died." He paused as he clicked on one and opened it bigger. "Yes, see, right here. *'I have been astonished that Men could die Martyrs for religion – I have shudder'd at it – I shudder no more – I could be martyr'd for my Religion – Love is my religion – I could die for that – I could die for you.'*" Lawrence read an excerpt from the email aloud. "That's Keats to Fanny Brawne."

Realisation hit Olivia and Dean at the same time.

"Francesca," they both exhaled.

17

"We can't be sure that it's Francesca just because her name is close to Fanny's," Olivia reasoned as they raced across town to the school. Lawrence had called Mr. Hargraves immediately after the duo had realised who the letters could be addressing. They were going to meet with Francesca once they arrived.

"Agreed," Lawrence replied. "Still, it would be an incredible coincidence if it was someone else. He's an English teacher, after all."

"True," Olivia responded. "Let's just make sure we keep an open mind. Just in case."

Lawrence hummed in agreement. The pair had gotten so caught up in the whirlwind of discovery that they hadn't had any time to process his absence the past day and a half, and as the silence crept into the car, so too did the knowledge that eventually they would have to address it.

"So," Lawrence started, gently glancing over to Olivia before returning his gaze to the road. "What else did I miss?"

We're going to keep on ignoring it, then, Olivia thought dejectedly to herself. She wasn't sure why she expected anything more, but that didn't lessen the sting she felt.

"Mostly just checking facts and confirming records," she replied, choosing not to look at Lawrence as she spoke. "I spoke with Lydia Fisher's sister, Margaret Anderson. She confirmed that Lydia went to bed around 9pm on the night of the murder, although I'm not sure how much I trust her. She seems like she'd lie for Lydia in a heartbeat. Plus, Our Lyds could have always snuck out."

Lawrence nodded at that explanation, eyes firmly on the road as he came to a junction.

"I recorded it in case you'd like to listen to it," she offered, aware she was probably talking too much. "My guess is that Lydia didn't kill Simon, but I don't think Margaret's corroboration makes her alibi rock solid. If this case has proven anything, it's that people will do wild things for love."

"Indeed," Lawrence agreed. "Simon's life was full of secrets, after all."

"You can say that again," Olivia sighed. "Also, Dr. James finalised the autopsy report. It was intense overkill, possibly with a blunt object. The body was surprisingly clean of evidence from the killer, which he made sure to note. It doesn't usually fit with a passionate murder like this one. Still, it'll help prove that this was premeditated. Dr. James *did* find a long blonde hair, though."

"And Francesca's a brunette," Lawrence added.

His comment hung in the car for a moment.

"You really think a small fifteen-year-old girl is capable of heaving a man as large as Simon Fisher off of a balcony?" Olivia asked, incredulously turning to her partner.

"Not necessarily," he replied. "But do I think we should rule out her involvement right away? No." He met Olivia's stare briefly. "And it's possible that at the end of the brutal attack, something made Simon jump."

Olivia settled back into her seat.

"I *highly* doubt that," she answered.

"I didn't say *probable*. Just possible," Lawrence bristled.

Olivia debated responding but couldn't think of anything adequate to say.

The knowledge that they were eventually going to have to settle their fight from Monday once again seeped into the car, becoming increasingly obvious with each passing second.

"So," Lawrence exhaled, eyes locked on the road. "Do you want to talk about it?"

"Do *I* want to talk about it?" Olivia demanded, whirling to face her partner. "Funny of you to just walk in after almost two days and act like nothing's wrong *and then* ask if *I* want to talk about it."

Annoyance coated Olivia's voice with each new word. She hadn't planned for things to get so heated, but it was getting ridiculous now. The real elephant in the room was the fact that her partner had buggered off at something so trivial. He'd heard what Francesca had said. He'd heard her words that were dipped in poison, and Olivia had apologised profusely. Dragging it on any longer than necessary was bordering on childish.

She took a deep breath and mentally counted to ten.

"It's a simple question, Liv," Lawrence replied evenly. His calm attitude made Olivia's blood boil even more.

"You can be so infuriating sometimes, you know that?" she groaned. She hadn't thought this far ahead in all of her ponderings about this moment. She'd been focused on getting Lawrence back, not on the hard conversations they would need to have after. Or how difficult he could make things.

Lawrence flexed his arms against the steering wheel.

"I know," he replied, voice quiet.

Olivia turned out toward the window, watching the houses and people as they drove past. The pause in their conversation gave her a moment to gather her thoughts and process everything slowly.

"Listen, Lawrence," she started, after feeling the annoyance dissolve slightly. "I understand why you were upset with me. I went too far. I get it. Why *I'm* upset is that you left me out to dry. And even if you're mad at me, *we*," she gestured between them, "are still a team. And I need to know that you've still got my back. You can't just abandon me in the middle of a case!" Her rant sat in the air, hanging over the two detectives like a storm cloud.

She heard him take a long slow breath.

"I've got your back," Lawrence replied after a moment of silence. "I waited to come back until I knew that I could do it. I didn't want to pretend like I was okay with everything when I wasn't. And I'll be better about not dropping everything in our professional life if we have an argument again."

Olivia nodded.

"I guess I just want to understand *why* it came to this," she said. "Why did it affect you so much that you had to lie about being sick just to avoid me?"

Lawrence shook his head, and for a moment she thought he wasn't going to answer. Instead, he pulled the car over to the side of the road and turned to her. His brows were furrowed in an expression she hadn't seen before.

"What is it," Olivia asked.

He ran a hand through his hair and exhaled deeply.

"Five years ago," he started, "as a DC, I was with my DI out talking to a young woman. She thought her stalker was the same guy suspected of murder. She was a little bitch, there's no denying it, but we had a job to do and a duty to her. Honestly, she was vile, but I understood that behind it all, she was damaged. My DI laid into her. Really gave it all out. Everything got..." He paused, and Olivia reached out to touch his arm.

"Go on..." she encouraged.

He nodded slowly.

"Ah... I still remember it fresh on my mind," he responded. "This DI, you might remember him... His family died in that fire. DI Wayne. Well, this girl said some shit about how he should have died in the fire too, and he fucking lost it. Grabbed her, I mean. It just went bad, and I had to break him away…and he lost his job, of course. But the worst part? The girl killed herself that night. Thought that if the police couldn't help her, no one could."

"God..." Olivia sighed. "I mean, that's just bloody awful."

Lawrence hummed.

"It is...*was*," he agreed. "So, when I saw what happened with you, it brought it all back, and then the tension and the thinking... I got this migraine, and I know it sounds stupid, but I just couldn't do that again. It can't happen."

Olivia watched the expression on his face.

"Dean, I'm..." She tried to think of a better thing to say but came up short. "I'm so sorry. *Really* sorry. Honestly, I am. I had no idea..."

She could understand it now and see why her reaction had thrown him over the edge and why he needed space.

She squeezed his arm.

"I *promise* this won't happen again," Olivia reassured him. She let out a shallow breath as Francesca's words entered her mind, reminding her of just how cutting they had been. "And even if I do get angry again, I'll walk out. I won't lash out on a victim, let alone a child."

"Good," Lawrence replied. He let his eyes meet with hers for the first time since he'd pulled over. "Because if you do it again, I may be out of this partnership for good."

I may be out of this partnership for good. The words lurked in Olivia's mind as she followed Mr. Hargraves to the meeting room. She knew he'd meant it, too and it shocked her that Lawrence was so ready to cut and run.

I've got this, she told herself. *You're cool, calm, and collected. And no teenager is going to change that*, she promised herself. She glanced at Lawrence, who strode down the halls with a quiet confidence, no hint of their earlier argument present in his body language. *Does it hurt you like it hurts me?* she wanted to ask him, but she couldn't bring herself to rouse up that scar tissue. They needed to focus on the case, not on their squabble, even if she thought they may need a bit more of a resolution.

"Miss Atkinson will be in shortly," Mr. Hargraves told the detectives before closing the door to the room.

Despite everything that had happened the last time, Francesca had insisted *'no snoops like Bev'* were allowed in to listen to her conversation. The head had been adamant on that fact, telling them the teen said she wouldn't see them if that were the case. After some toing and froing, they'd agreed the AA would stay in the corridor, and now, as they settled down at the end of a long table, Liv wondered what the girl was so afraid of revealing in front of someone.

"So, we know what we're doing?" Lawrence confirmed, looking to his partner.

She gave him a quick reassuring smile.

"Brilliant," he declared, settling into his chair with the gentle clearing of his throat. "As she won't have anyone in with her, we have to make sure we get enough written down to compare later."

Olivia nodded, folding herself into her own one.

The duo spent the next couple of minutes looking at their notes as they waited for Francesca to arrive. The silence, though slightly tense, was more comfortable this time. So much so that they barely noticed the figure of the teen as she appeared in the doorway, her arms crossed in silhouette.

"Francesca," Lawrence called out, standing. "Please, come in."

Liv stood also, joining her partner.

"What is *she* doing here?" Francesca demanded as she walked into the room, stopping as soon as she noticed Olivia.

"She's my partner, Francesca. She needs to be here,"

Lawrence encouraged, giving Olivia a look. "It's the rules. But you only have to talk to me,"

Liv bit her lip to stop herself from saying anything. Francesca still looked wary.

"She can apologise if you'd like," Lawrence offered. "Or just sit in the back of the room and observe. You can pretend like she's not even here."

The teen looked between the two detectives, indecision playing across her features.

"I want you to apologise," she declared finally, crossing her arms again. Her eyebrows raised and lowered quickly in a challenge.

Olivia took a deep breath. It was harder than she thought to swallow down everything the young girl had said and apologise. She could feel Dean's eyes on her. The weight of his past experiences hanging on her shoulders.

"I'm sorry for yelling at you, Francesca," Olivia spoke, keeping her words slow and her voice quiet. "It was unprofessional and inappropriate, and I promise it won't happen again. As soon as I realised what happened, I regretted it, and I hope you accept my apology."

That seemed to do the trick, as Miss Atkinson flounced into a chair after giving Olivia another look. It was very much on the smug side, but at least it was behind them for now.

"Good!" Lawrence said, pleased that nothing more had come from the mini incident. "Mind if we start?"

"Whatever." She sighed, playing with her nails.

"Okay, right," he did his best to keep his voice calm, almost sweet, and Olivia admired that. It took some strength to rise above a brat. "We really appreciate you meeting with us again and understand that you didn't want to have your parents or any adults present. Partially because of that, we think you know some things that may be extremely helpful in the investigation into Mr. Fisher's murder."

Francesca seemed to freeze at that, her attempt at ambivalence evaporating. It was a clever smokescreen while it lasted, but she wasn't terribly good at maintaining it.

"You...you didn't say murder at the assembly," she commented, voice a bit shaky.

Lawrence nodded.

"We didn't want to alarm the whole school," he offered. "Plus, we didn't have confirmation back from the medical examiner. But now that we do, it's even more important we understand what Mr. Fisher was like. Who disliked him? If he had any enemies..." Lawrence paused for dramatic effect between each sentence. Francesca huffed at the enemies comment, prompting Dean to lean in closer, hands folded in front of him.

"Do you know if he had any enemies, Francesca?" he asked, attempting to meet her gaze.

She shifted awkwardly.

"How should I know?" The tone of her question fell

flat, and Lawrence raised an eyebrow at her. "No, no enemies," she added with a deep breath, her leg bouncing quickly as she lifted and lowered her heel against the ground.

Nervous tick, Olivia wanted to say, but she kept her mouth shut. They had agreed that she wouldn't speak unless Francesca directly addressed her.

"Understood," Lawrence commented, making a point to write in his notepad.

"Except for maybe his wife," Francesca piped up, unable to refrain from elaborating.

"His wife?" Lawrence asked, quirking his head.

The girl nodded.

"Yeah, he hated her," she answered. "They'd stopped living together." A daring smile accompanied her commentary.

Lawrence nodded as he continued to write in his notebook. He was a good actor, that much Olivia had become increasingly aware of throughout their partnership.

"You seem to know a lot about Mr. Fisher. Were you two close?" he asked, looking up at the end of his question to meet Francesca's eyes.

She fidgeted.

"Not really. I just enjoy gossip," she replied, twirling a strand of hair through her fingertips. "Makes a boring class get interesting."

The girl bit the corner of her lip, a trait that Olivia

took to mean she was either trying to keep from crying or trying to keep the truth from spilling out.

"Where did you hear that Mrs. Fisher had stopped living at their shared flat?" Dean continued to probe. Even though his questions were more pointed, he didn't let it affect his tone of voice. He remained calm—though not overconfident—even as he started to corner Francesca into her own lie. It was impressive to watch.

"Loads of people knew." She sighed, pretending to sound bored. "It wasn't like he hid it well. Listen, I don't understand how this is helping you solve the case."

"That's fair," Lawrence shot back. "You were in Mr. Fisher's poetry class, correct?"

Francesca nodded wordlessly.

"Have you studied the poet, John Keats?"

Francesca jolted forward in her chair at the question, unable to contain a physical response. She cleared her throat. *She's sweating*, Olivia noticed. *You know we're going to get there, sweetheart. Just tell us now.*

"Yeah, we might have talked about Keats in class," she replied, extra acidity melding into her voice. "He was one of the Romantics. Real tragic and all that. Don't get how that's relevant to Mr. Fisher's death. Just a dead poet."

Although Francesca tried to act disinterested, Olivia could see that her breathing had quickened. They were closing in.

"I think you do know how Keats is relevant, though,"

Lawrence replied, calling Francesca's bluff. She swallowed.

C'mon, kid, Olivia wanted to say. *Just give it up.*

Instead, the teen simply shook her head. She was clearly rattled.

"Francesca," Lawrence sighed, sympathy washing over his features. "We know about Bright Star."

Her eyes widened as Lawrence uttered the alias Mr. Fisher used to court his victim.

"Wha—I don't know what you're talking about," she fumbled over her words. She couldn't look him in the eye. "What's that?"

"You know, Francesca. I know you do," Lawrence urged, leaning so far forward Olivia thought he might fall out of his chair.

"Please stop." Her plead was barely above a whisper, tears threatening to streak down her cheeks. It had never been so abundantly clear to Olivia that this was a child they were speaking with. It built a rage deep in her stomach that their victim would hurt someone as young and fragile as Francesca. Even with her attitude, she was still a young woman, just learning how to operate in the world. The fact that a grown adult would prey on her sickened Olivia. Teachers were supposed to help students, not hunt them.

"You know that I can't just stop, Francesca." Lawrence's voice sounded like a concession, even as he pressed her further. "You were Bright Star, weren't you?"

Tears flooded to Francesca's eyes, and she let out a wail that shocked Olivia, coming from such a small body. She sounded like a wounded bird. She buried her head in her hands, silent sobs wracking her shoulders.

"Francesca, I'm so sorry," Lawrence spoke quietly. "He shouldn't have done that to you."

"What do you mean, he shouldn't have done that?" Rage bubbled over Francesca's voice, cutting through her cries. "I love him... He *loved* me."

Olivia winced at the declaration. She wanted to rush over to the teen, to assure her that grown men shouldn't be in love with children, that with time she'd realise the situation for what it was. But she couldn't. She had agreed with Lawrence to let him lead.

"Forgive me," Lawrence backtracked. "I hadn't realised..."

"Of *course* you wouldn't have known," Francesca sobbed, head still buried between her arms. Despite being unable to see the girl's face, Olivia knew that it was probably a mess. She knew what it was like to cry that hard, and it was never pretty. "Our love was special." The second statement was quiet, almost an ode.

"When did this start?" Lawrence asked quietly, finally lowering his gaze to his notepad and away from the girl. *Smart*, Olivia thought. *Let her feel the pressure relax.*

"We started writing a year ago after he had to cover my class. At first, that's all it was," Francesca started to explain. She let her head emerge from between her arms but kept her gaze downcast. "I'd ask him about a poet or a verse, and he'd explain them to me." She smiled as she recalled it.

Olivia had to turn away; she couldn't stand to look at Francesca as she recounted the beginning of her abuse.

"Then we started talking about our lives," the teen continued. "How I want to be a poet when I'm older. How he's finishing his novel. Stuff like that. We decided we'd grab coffee after school one weekend and realised we were like old souls."

Lawrence looked back at Olivia; his face was as pained as hers was.

We have to let her continue to talk, she urged with her body language. Lawrence gave a defeated nod.

"I was the one who initiated a relationship," Francesca declared, finally looking up to meet both detectives' gazes. "I swear on my nan's grave. He didn't touch me until I had practically forced myself onto him."

Olivia's stomach lurched. It was painful to hear Francesca romanticise it all.

"We knew we had to keep it a secret. That the world wouldn't understand that this was *love*, not some creepy teacher perving on his student."

Olivia shook her head. *That's exactly what this is, sweetheart*, she wanted to say.

She bit her tongue instead.

"We agreed that we'd wait until I started uni to make it official." Francesca explained. "That until then we were just going to go about our lives as if nothing had changed." Her eyes shone with passion—and tears—as she spoke.

"Did anyone else know about the relationship?" Lawrence asked, interrupting Francesca's soliloquy.

She shook her head.

"We swore to never tell a soul," she explained. "Even when he ended things with his wife, he said it just wasn't working for him to be married to her."

Lawrence glanced at Olivia again. *He told her he was the one who broke things off. Sick bastard.*

Francesca sniffed.

"When in reality," she continued. "He just couldn't stand to be with her while he was committed to *me*."

Lawrence wrote that down too.

"Not even your parents knew?" he pressed, searching for any explanation that someone knew of the affair. "They didn't suspect anything?"

Francesca shook her head.

"My parents are too busy chasing their careers and hating each other to notice what their middle child is doing," she seethed.

Olivia made a mental note that the young teen was clearly neglected at home. She was the perfect recipe for an abuser.

"Francesca, this is particularly important. It might help us figure out who killed Mr. Fisher," Lawrence urged. "You're sure *no one* else knew?"

"Positive," she replied, face crumpling as she said it. "And I wish you would stop acting like our relationship would be enough of a reason for someone to—to *hurt* Simon." Her sobs started anew at that comment.

Lawrence looked to Olivia, who simply shrugged. Francesca seemed to be telling the truth; that much was certain. They let her cry, waiting to see if she'd say anything else.

"Simon made me feel so special," she blurted out through her sobs, drawing the detectives' attention back to her.

"I know that right now it feels like your love for him is the only thing holding you to this earth," Olivia said before her internal monologue could warn her against it. The girl glanced up, seemingly affronted that Olivia spoke but also wanting words of encouragement. It was all Olivia needed. "But I promise you that that's not the case. You're strong, and you're your own person, and this next while is going to be difficult, but I think you're going to get through it just fine. In fact, I *know* it. I have a counsellor I trust that I think you should consider giving a visit to. She's helped me through loss before."

There was silence in the room for a moment, and Olivia caught Lawrence looking at her, the expression on his face thanking her for adding in the warmth.

"What do you know about loss?" Francesca wailed, wiping tears away as she spoke. "People always pretend to know everything, but no one will know what this feels like!"

Lawrence gave Olivia a gentle nod, encouraging her to tell her story.

"My partner was killed," Olivia confessed gently. "And you know what? It still hurts every single day. But I'm able to get out of bed now and keep going. I even make it through most days without crying about him now. And it doesn't mean I don't miss him. I miss him desperately, in fact. But I've learned that he wouldn't want me to live my life for him instead of for me."

The last sentence sunk into herself deeper than she'd intended. She always knew that, but saying it out loud gave her strength and made her realise that she hadn't been doing that.

"I don't ever want to get over him," Francesca whimpered, pulling her blazer tighter around her. "I just want him back."

Olivia thought about telling her that she wouldn't always want him back, that one day she'd realise that Simon Fisher was a predator. Just a common abuser, not the love of her life. That one day she'd meet a boy—or maybe a girl—who took her breath away and that she'd begin to heal. That when she was older, she'd understand that near-middle-aged teachers shouldn't be going after fifteen-year-olds. That one day she'd be angry at Mr. Fisher, not missing him.

Instead, she swallowed her pride and gave the child a sympathetic nod.

"It's hard. But this counsellor—or any counsellor, really—can help you process your grief. It's really important that you do that," Olivia urged. "We can set you up with one."

"I'll think about it," Francesca muttered, looking down to her hands.

Olivia looked back to Lawrence as she crossed the threshold to soothingly rub the teen's arm.

He seemed unsettled at Francesca's adamance that she was in love. A pang of gratitude shot through Olivia as she realised he didn't seem upset with her; in fact, if anything he was giving her a look of admiration.

"It's okay to be sad," Olivia reassured her as she settled back in her seat. "I promise."

Francesca sniffled but nodded as she stared at the scuffed tiled floor.

"If it's all right with you, we'd like to drive you home," Lawrence offered, standing to grab his coat. "Make sure that you make it back safely and all that."

"But it's only partway through the school day," Francesca replied, confusion dancing across her face.

"Indeed. But we'll speak with Mr. Hargraves to make sure you're excused," Lawrence assured her, passing Olivia her coat. She took it with a gentle smile. They were building their trust back, slowly but surely.

"I don't understand," Francesca stuttered, looking from one detective to the other. "Why can't I just finish my day?"

"We'd like to speak with your parents briefly, Francesca," Lawrence admitted, leading the way to the door.

She raced to Dean, panic in her eyes.

"No, you can't tell them," she blurted out. "They'd— please, please don't tell them."

Lawrence gave her a long look before sighing.

"I think telling them now would be the right thing to do," he explained, trying to maintain a calm tone. "Something like this... We have to help them understand what happened and why. Abuse..."

"It wasn't abuse! It was love!" Francesca interjected, now physically clinging to Lawrence's arm. He gently tried to release her hand, but she was desperate.

"Francesca," he urged. "Please, let's not make this any harder than it has to be."

Sobs wracked through the teen's body as she crumpled into Lawrence. Slowly, he lowered his hand down and comforted her. He looked slightly awkward doing so, but the softer side suited him.

"Why is the entire world against me?" Francesca wailed.

Dean hesitantly gave her a gentle squeeze before extricating himself from her grasp. Olivia deftly swooped in, grabbing the teen and pulling her into an embrace.

"It's going to be okay," she urged, brushing her hair out of her dewy eyes. "I promise it'll be okay. We'll do it in the kindest way possible, and we'll let you decide if you want to be there or not."

"I—" Francesca choked on the word, another cry consuming her body. "I think I want to be the one to tell them," she managed to say. "I want it to come from me."

"Of course," Olivia promised, giving the young woman a squeeze before stepping back to let her have her own space.

"Right," Lawrence said taking out his phone. "I'll call your parents and ask them to meet us at your house. Would you mind giving Liv directions?"

Francesca nodded, clearly numb.

"That's great," Olivia encouraged. "That's really great."

What have we gotten ourselves into? she asked herself. *And who the hell killed Simon Fisher?*

18

Francesca Atkinson's family home was more of a mansion than a house. Olivia did her best not to gawk as they approached the front door. The teenager had done her best to try and clean up during their car ride, but they could still sense the apprehension from her.

It made sense; Olivia couldn't imagine having to tell her parents what Francesca was about to disclose.

"Are your parents in, do you think?" Lawrence asked as they knocked on the large oak door. They hadn't been able to reach them by phone despite several attempts on the way over.

Francesca nodded, obscuring her face behind her long brown hair.

"They both work from home, so yeah," she affirmed, playing with the sleeves of her coat. "They're probably both in meetings or something."

Lawrence knocked again.

"Well, we're going to have to speak with them," he sighed.

Before Francesca had the chance to respond, the door swung open to reveal a petite woman with deep brown hair pulled into a sleek high ponytail. Mrs. Atkinson was the epitome of clean lines and a sharp silhouette, a woman who oozed business and seriousness. She stood there for a moment in her tight yet professional dark blue dress, arms crossed before reaching to her headset. Her hawkish gaze seemed to discern every detail of the scene in front of her. There were no questions in her eyes.

"Can I call you back in a minute, Joe?" Her voice was crisp and to the point, even at a whisper. The stranger she was speaking to evidently agreed, because she pressed a button before peeling the sleek earpiece off and finally turning to fully address the trio.

"What on earth has Francesca done this time?" She addressed Lawrence as she asked the question, annoyance tingeing her words.

No wonder the girl felt like her parents didn't care, Olivia thought to herself.

"Ma'am, I'm Detective Inspector Lawrence with Devon and Cornwall Police." He held up his badge. "This is my partner, Detective Inspector Austin." He kept an impressively tactful tone as he addressed the woman. "Please, may we step inside?"

Francesca's mother wordlessly pulled the door

further open, welcoming the detectives into a grandiose foyer. A grand staircase trailed up into the next floor, presumably sequestering bedrooms and the discretion of private life. She gestured, still silent, to a drawing room off to the side.

"Thank you," Lawrence muttered as they walked to sit down.

Fran followed behind, refusing to meet her mother's eye.

"I'm presuming that you're Francesca's mother?" he asked once everyone was inside the room.

"Correct," she agreed, glaring at her daughter. "Please, I assure you whatever damage Fannie may have caused, we can pay for it. We don't need—"

"Ma'am, is your husband here as well?" Lawrence ignored the comments. Mrs. Atkinson almost looked shocked.

"I—Yes, he is, but I promise this is something I can take care of on my own."

Dean glanced at Olivia before looking back at Francesca. The girl, all rage and spitfire at school, was doing her best to make herself as small as possible.

"Ma'am, with all due respect, it's important we talk with you *both*," Lawrence enunciated.

Olivia knew her partner well enough to hear the gentlest of strain in his voice.

"Really, it isn't necessary," Mrs. Atkinson insisted with a dismissive wave of her hand. She glanced down to her phone and quickly started texting.

"Ma'am." Lawrence's tone turned dark. "I *insist*. This isn't what you think it is."

Olivia saw a flicker of confusion for the first time on Mrs. Atkinson's face. She hid it quickly and effectively, but it had undeniably happened.

"One moment," she muttered. "I'll go and fetch him." She whisked herself out of the drawing room before the sentence had fully left her mouth. Lawrence looked to Francesca.

"Are you okay?" he asked, his voice already gentler.

She shrugged.

"I still don't think you need to tell them," she whispered. "It's not like they care, anyway."

"You know that's not how it works, Francesca," Lawrence assured her. "Are you still up for telling them? Otherwise, we can do it."

The teenager shook her head at that offer.

"I need to be the one," she insisted, fresh tears brimming in her eyes.

"Understood," Lawrence agreed as he looked to Olivia. She gave him a gentle smile.

Moments later Mrs. Atkinson entered the room trailed by a similarly short balding man in a crisp grey suit.

The detectives stood.

"Mr. Atkinson, I'm DI Lawrence, this is DI Austin," Lawrence started, reaching out his hand to introduce himself. The man took his grip firmly. "We need to speak with you and your wife on a few matters."

A tense silence momentarily settled amongst the room.

"This better be important, to pull me from a board meeting," Francesca's father muttered.

"I'm afraid it is," Lawrence sighed. "Please, if you both could have a seat."

The Atkinsons begrudgingly settled into a loveseat opposite the detectives, Francesca sitting in a small chair on her own.

"Your daughter has something that she's going to share with you," Lawrence started, looking at the teen who continued to hide behind her brown hair.

"Fannie, what's happened?"

Olivia couldn't tell if it was concern or impatience in Mrs. Atkinson's voice. *Probably both*, she thought to herself. How often did these adults actually *speak* with their children?

"I, uh," Francesca started, continuing to keep her face downcast. Her eyes darted back and forth between her hands.

She's trying to figure out how to say it, Olivia thought, her heart going out to the child.

"The teacher who died earlier this week—Mr. Fisher —he—" Francesca choked over the words, burying her head in her hands before finishing her thought.

Olivia kept her eyes tracked on Francesca's parents as she spoke, watching for any reaction that would imply they knew already.

Mrs. Atkinson's back straightened at the mention of

Mr. Fisher's name. Mr. Atkinson did his best to stay engaged, but confusion was clearly written across his face.

"Do I have to?" Francesca asked, looking to Lawrence.

He gave her a gentle nod.

"It's okay, Francesca," he urged, offering the gentlest lilt of a smile.

She wiped the tears from her cheeks with the back of her sleeve, cleared her throat, and stared directly at her mother.

"Mr. Fisher and I were in love," Francesca stated, her voice strong until it cracked at the end, revealing the crumbling emotional state behind her brave face.

"I don't—I don't understand," Mr. Atkinson spoke, glancing from Francesca to each detective before looking back at his daughter. "What do you mean, darling?"

"What do I mean?" Francesca spat out, eyes narrowing with rage. Tears continued to flow freely down her face as she animated into the angry teen from earlier. The word *vengeful* barely seemed to encapsulate the fury in her voice as she confronted her parents.

"I *mean* that we were in love! Head over heels, fucking like rabbits, making promises to grow old together...in love!"

The Atkinsons, at first mildly uncomfortable, sat with jaws agape at Francesca's outburst.

"Fannie!" Mrs. Atkinson breathed, eyes wide with

bewilderment. "Fannie, Mr. Fisher is—was twenty years your senior. And he dared to put his hands on you? You should have told us."

"Like you'd even listen," Francesca cried, refusing to look at either parent.

"You don't know that, darling. We listen *all* the time," Mrs. Atkinson insisted, standing to go to her daughter's side. She elegantly folded herself onto the floor despite her tight dress, taking Francesca's hands in her own as she looked up at her. "Even if sometimes we can seem busy or distracted. If you ever need to tell us something—we're here."

Francesca pulled her hands away, pushing herself further into the chair.

"Detectives, thank you for bringing this to our attention," Mrs. Atkinson said, turning to face Lawrence and Olivia. Despite the sincerity painted on her face, Olivia couldn't help but feel as if it was a calculated move. Prove concern. Portray the perfect family they all knew had gaping cracks in need of mending.

"Fannie—I'm so sorry," Mr. Atkinson spoke for the first time since she broke the news. He shook his head gently. "I'm so sorry."

Olivia's line of work meant she saw adult men cry more than the average Brit, but it wasn't very frequently that she saw a man fully break down in front of her. That was the best word to describe Mr. Atkinson in the moment, however. He buried his head in his hands—so much like his daughter—as his shoulders were wracked with large sobs.

"Mr. and Mrs. Atkinson," Olivia addressed them directly for the first time. "I know this has been a shocking revelation, but we need to ask what everyone in the household was doing on Saturday evening."

Mr. Atkinson continued to sob.

"We were all in the house," Mrs. Atkinson insisted, still at her daughter's feet. "I want to resent the implication that we could have anything to do with Mr. Fisher's demise—I'm assuming that's why you're asking, anyway—but if that criminal was still alive, I'd probably be hunting him down this very moment." Rage boiled in her voice.

"Don't say that," Francesca whimpered. "Please."

Olivia winced as she reflected on the amount of brainwashing that the poor teen was going to have to grapple with in the coming months.

"I mean it. You're a child, for fuck's sake," Mrs. Atkinson ranted, her face going through three or four emotions in the span of seconds. Rage. Despair. Confusion. "A grown man has no business involving himself with you!"

A phone, somewhere in the house, rang, but everyone chose to ignore it.

"This was *different!*" Francesca insisted, practically yelling. "When we were together, it wasn't about age."

Olivia watched as the girl's hands squeezed the arms of her chair.

"We have a security alarm system that tracks all coming and going from the house, as well as video cameras at all entrances." Mr. Atkinson's disembodied voice interrupted the conflict between mother and daughter, his eyes glazed over. "I can have the company send over our records from Saturday to Sunday. I trust you'll find we all stayed in the house for the evening."

Olivia and Lawrence shared a long glance.

"That would be most helpful, Mr. Atkinson," Lawrence chimed in. He pulled out a business card and set it on one of the end tables. "Our contact information is on that card. We'll be in touch with details of counsellors for her, should you choose to go down that route. We highly recommend it. Is there anything else we can do to support you all in this moment?"

Francesca pulled her hair back from her face. The heartbreak etched on her face was clearly eating her alive inside.

Mrs Atkinson was the first to speak.

"Is there any—any justice that we can get for our Fannie?" she asked. It was the closest she seemed to be to crying since the truth had come out.

"Unfortunately, I'm not sure there is," Lawrence sighed. "Unless we can prove that the school knew and neglected to take action."

"No one knew," Francesca growled. "And I don't want there to be anything else that happens—isn't Simon's death enough?" By the time she had finished the sentence, her voice had returned to a wail.

Olivia took her notepad out and wrote down the number of her therapist.

"Here's the number of a counsellor whom I trust," she offered. "I know we were going to give you a list, but this one really knows her stuff. I think it would be a good idea to have Francesca see her, as well as possibly considering family therapy. An event like this is traumatic and can put strain on relationships."

Francesca scoffed; Mrs. Atkinson did her best not to roll her eyes.

"We'll do it." Mr. Atkinson's voice was quiet but carried all of the weight needed to end the conversation. "And I'll make sure the security company gets that information to you as quickly as possible. Is there anything else you need, detectives?"

Olivia was a little startled at the haste in which he was ready to wrap everything up. For a moment, she'd been convinced the girl's father was devastated at the news. Now, however, she wondered if it had all been an act to look as though he cared. Poor girl.

She quickly wrote her number down under the therapists one.

"My number's here too, Francesca," she assured her. "Please don't hesitate to reach out. It's hard, losing a loved one." Her relationship with Rhys was nothing like Francesca's affair with Simon. Still, she was sure the girl was feeling similar pain to her own right after she lost her partner.

Francesca's eyes darted to the paper, her lips pressed

tightly shut. Olivia didn't expect anything else. The girl would call if she felt it was necessary. She certainly couldn't force it, though.

"That should be all," Lawrence exhaled, standing as he spoke. Liv joined him. "We're okay to see ourselves out." The Atkinsons nodded; they were about to face their own storm. That didn't solve the detectives' mystery, however.

As the duo stepped into the cool afternoon air, Lawrence gave out a long sigh. Olivia chuckled.

"You can say that again," she muttered as they walked toward the car. "Both parents reacted with shock. Mrs. Atkinson was definitely performing a bit—but I don't think she knew about her daughter's affair."

"Agreed," Lawrence replied. "Which scratches some suspects out, but also brings us back to square one. We were so certain it was someone who knew that Francesca was being abused—where does that leave us now?" He shook his head ever so slightly as he looked around the Atkinson's drive.

"Let's get back to the station and see if anyone has some new leads," Olivia suggested.

"Sounds like a good idea," Lawrence chimed in, climbing into the car.

Olivia swiftly followed suit.

If not Francesca or her family, then who? Questions swirled in Olivia's head; she couldn't remember the last time she had been this perplexed by a case so far into the investigation.

Normally, the pieces slowly clicked into place, evidence by evidence, revealing a cohesive picture. This time, however, it felt like they were expecting a whole different puzzle than the one they had found themselves with, like someone had swapped the boxes.

As the detectives sped off into the distance, all Olivia could hope was that they figured out what the true picture was soon enough.

19

Clara flounced into the station, her bright green jumpsuit standing out amidst the sea of people in shades of greys and browns. Her steps always had a lightness to them, as though she were walking on clouds instead of drab tile.

"You called?" she asked as she waltzed into Olivia and Lawrence's office. The pair had just arrived back and were in the midst of unpacking their belongings.

"Clara!" Olivia exclaimed as she looked up to see the tech analyst. A warm smile spread across her often-stoic features. "So glad you could come over."

"Agreed," Lawrence chimed in, mild-mannered as always. That earned him a cheeky smile from Clara, who swung herself up onto Olivia's desk.

"Careful," Olivia chided, although her tone made it clear that she was mostly joking. "I was surprised to hear you were in. What happened to the races?"

Clara pulled her tablet from her pastel pink bag and switched the screen on.

"Really, it's a long story to do with tickets, misunderstandings, and a dirty burger that in my opinion was massively undercooked." She rolled her eyes for emphasis while the detectives glanced at each other. "Anyway... what's the word on the Fisher case?" she asked. One of her braids fell forward, and she swooped the whole lot of them back, tying them against each other into a large bun.

"To be completely honest...we're stuck." Olivia sighed, settling into her chair. Lawrence did the same at his own desk. "We thought the killer would be linked to Fisher's student victim in some way...maybe her father or older brother. But after interviewing her, it's clear that no one knew about the so-called affair except for the victim and Simon."

"And the wife," Lawrence added, giving Olivia a pointed look.

"And the wife," Olivia agreed. She seemed hesitant to say anything more than that. "So, I guess we were wondering if you found any more red flags—even yellow flags at this point—with Fisher's digital footprint."

"Got it," Clara agreed, pulling up her file on Simon Fisher as Olivia spoke. "Well, I can tell you one thing: he didn't seem to have any other victims. At least not any that he had correspondence with. But that seems to be what he really liked about it—getting to talk about himself." Olivia could hear the disdain in Clara's voice; it paralleled the bitter taste on her own tongue.

"Is there perhaps a forum he may have gotten involved with online—somewhere where he could have shared that he was instigating a relationship with a fifteen-year-old?"

Clara shook her head at Olivia's question.

"It was worth a shot," she acquiesced.

"What about something that doesn't have anything to do with the affair at all?" Lawrence asked, perking up. "Debt, perhaps. Or ties to a gang?"

Clara gave him a loaded look at that question.

"You really think Mr. English teacher Simon Fisher was involved with a *gang*?" Sarcasm cut her words, searing the room with heat.

"Well, not necessarily a *gang*, but—someone unsavoury," Lawrence replied, throwing his hands up in the air in defeat. "Right now, we have next to nothing to go on, so anything that might help would be terrific."

The three of them sat in silent contemplation for a moment.

"The man was fairly strait-laced," Clara replied, scrolling through the file on her tablet. "I've been doing some digging into his wife, Lydia. I know she has an alibi, but she just seems too *clean*. If she could hate him enough to stand over his squished body on the pavement with no emotion, then she's capable of killing him. She had every motive to, right?"

Olivia perked up as Clara went through the laundry

list of reasons why Mrs. Fisher could still be their suspect.

"What if it isn't about Simon at all?" she asked, looking at Lawrence. He clearly had the same cogs turning in his mind. "What if it's about Lydia? Someone trying to send a message to her—warn her."

"Do what needs to be done or you're next," Lawrence agreed, fumbling to stand.

"It could have even been someone who thought Lydia was at the flat. It wasn't massively public knowledge that they were living separately," Olivia continued, eyes widening. "The overkill could be because they were furious that the woman herself wasn't around."

Lawrence rubbed at the stubble on the side of his face.

"Damnit, we need to speak to her again." He decided.

Olivia nodded enthusiastically, already grabbing for her coat. She watched her partner put his phone and keys into his pocket quickly.

"Thank you for everything, Clara," Olivia called out to the tech analyst who hopped down from her desk.

"No, you're welcome," Clara replied in a sing-song voice. "Just doing my job. I'm back in the office from now, so just give me bell if you need me!"

Lawrence appeared at her side, ducking in to give her a brief kiss on the cheek before grabbing his own coat.

"You're brilliant," he affirmed.

She laughed heartily as she put her belongings back into her pink bag and flung it over her shoulder.

"You best know it," she confirmed with a smirk. "Now, have fun storming the castle!"

They said their goodbyes, and Clara disappeared from their office. They could hear her voice as she stopped to speak to the other detectives.

Olivia pulled together the items she had *just* sprawled every which way in haste. Mentally making sure she hadn't forgotten anything. *Phone, keys, purse, notepad.*

"Ready?" Lawrence asked, poised by the door.

She nodded, adrenalin at the thought they might finally be getting somewhere coursed through her veins.

The duo whisked themselves off into the hallway, any rift from arguments earlier in the week scabbing over to allow their synchronicity to resume. Even their steps moved like those marching in a well-oiled battalion. Olivia was struck with a comforting hope that perhaps they could heal the divide from their argument. She knew it wouldn't be easy, but striding next to her partner, she had a sense that it was entirely possible—probable, even.

Relief flooded her senses at that realisation. *It's going to be okay.*

20

Margaret Anderson's home was quaint, unassuming. Looking upon it, Olivia realised it would be quite the place to hide away from the world. The memories of Lydia recounting her month of depression and absence from the comings and goings of everyday life suddenly made much more sense, gazing upon the small brick building with its welcoming windows.

Lawrence had called Lydia on their drive over, allowing Olivia to get behind the wheel in a somewhat rare—but not altogether unseen—role reversal. *We're figuring out our boundaries of trust again*, Olivia had thought to herself as she drove toward the location of their victim's wife. Lydia had answered and replied that both she and Margaret were indeed home.

The woman looked as pale as a ghost as she opened the door for the detectives. They exchanged brief pleasantries before winding up in Margaret's lounge, the detectives seated across from the sisters.

Margaret looked shockingly similar to Lydia; both women had rather petite frames, though sinews of muscle rippling under their skin. Mrs. Fisher's stormy eyes matched her sister's perfectly.

"I'll put the kettle on," Margaret half whispered with a warm smile before whisking herself off to the nearby kitchen.

With a moment to be alone, Olivia turned to Lydia and offered her a reassuring smile.

"So, how have you been doing?" she asked, studying her face. Mrs. Fisher's gaze still seemed far off, as though she'd decided that existence in this world was too difficult, that another one would be much easier.

"I'm fine, detectives," she muttered, breaking her reverie to look down at her hands folded in her lap.

Olivia made a mental note to double check with Margaret once she returned from the kitchen.

"Okay, then," Lawrence sighed, settling back into the couch. "Thank you for meeting with us on such short notice."

"Of course," Lydia replied, again somehow far off although she sat right before them. "Have you found anything?" A glimmer of hope resided in her voice, searching for something.

Olivia wasn't sure if she even fully knew what it was that she was hoping for.

"We have made some progress on the case, but we

have yet to apprehend Mr. Fisher's killer," Lawrence conceded, choosing his words carefully.

Olivia gave him the subtlest of nods, impressed with his finesse.

"I understand," Lydia replied, biting her nails. "I hope you don't mind, but what brought you here? What can I help you with?"

There was a pause and the sound of rummaging in the cutlery drawer coming from the kitchen.

"Lydia," Olivia started, leaning in closer to the woman. "We're exploring the possibility that your husband was killed to get to you in some way. Do you know of anyone who may have wanted to hurt you? An ex-colleague who was mad, a debtor come to collect their debts, anyone who thinks you owe them something?"

Lydia's eyes widened as Olivia laid out her line of questioning. Her gaze darted frantically between the detectives.

"Well—what do you mean? I—" Every sentence she attempted to start died before she could finish it.

"Is there anyone you can think of that would want to hurt you, Lydia?" Olivia asked again, pressing on.

"Anyone who would want to hurt Lydia?" Margaret returned to the room as though on cue. "That's preposterous, isn't it?"

Lydia nodded slowly, looking to her sister as if she were a lifeline before she cleared her throat.

"Yes, there's not anyone who I can think of that

would…who would be that *angry* with me," she clarified, clearly more comfortable now that Margaret had returned to the room.

"No bitter exes or disgruntled neighbours? You're sure?" Lawrence's voice was soft, warm. He really did wonders with the women they interviewed Olivia noticed.

"I lead an uneventful life, I suppose," Lydia replied, stirring out of her stupor with each passing word. "I certainly have never had someone seriously threaten me before."

Lawrence nodded, and Olivia wrote it down as best she could while still appearing to listen.

"Has there been anything strange since your husband passed?" Dean continued once he was sure Olivia had everything written down. "Dead calls or cars driving by at an unusually slow pace?"

Lydia shook her head.

"Honestly, it's been very quiet here, detectives." She almost sounded a little irritated. At what, was anyone's guess, but she glanced up at her sister.

"I've certainly appreciated the calm," Margaret chimed in.

With her sister present, watching over her answers, Olivia figured it would be harder than anticipated to get the woman to let her guard down and open up.

"Have you thought of anything else since we last spoke?" she prodded. The kettle whistled from the kitchen, summoning Margaret from her perch. "Memories have a funny way of coming back to us sometimes."

Lydia made firm eye contact with Olivia.

"Not anything clear, no," she answered. "Although, the more I think about it—and everything haunts me—the more I'm positive his victim was a girl, not a boy."

Liv found herself remembering her own thoughts about *Giselle* from the first time she met the woman. *Which one are you?*

"That's definitely helpful, Lydia," Lawrence encouraged, though Olivia knew it was more to help Lydia feel comfortable speaking than anything else. "Any other information?"

The woman put her hand flat against her forehead.

"I just want to put this all behind me." Her words took on an eerie quality as she spoke, as though she were under a spell. "It's exhausting, having a murdered husband. Everyone is trying to comfort me, and all I want is to never think of him again."

A chill shot down Olivia's spine as Lydia spoke. She couldn't exactly blame her; she'd probably feel the same way if her dead husband had been an unrepentant paedophile. Still, the confession felt divorced of emotion, and that in and of itself was more startling than Lydia's words.

"We're hoping to conclude the case soon," Lawrence admitted as Margaret quietly returned to the lounge, a tray filled with a teapot and teacups balanced between her two hands.

"I hope Darjeeling is all right," she interjected, her grey eyes flashing up as she set the tea tray on the coffee table. "It's Lydia's favourite."

"Darjeeling sounds lovely," Olivia agreed, giving Margaret a gentle smile. The sister had been incredibly hospitable, almost at one with her abode.

Margaret's sincerity and ability to blend in had almost made Olivia become too settled where she was. If it hadn't been for the light, she may not have even noticed the dark purple bruise on Margaret's wrist, just below the cuff of her sleeve.

What does a gentle woman like Margaret do in order to get such a brutal bruise?

21

Olivia did her best to hide the fact that she'd noticed Margaret's bruise, desperately looking for something in her line of vision to comment on instead of the purple welt.

Her eyes landed on a portrait of Margaret smiling, arm wrapped around a vaguely familiar actress who beamed at the camera just as much.

"Margaret, is that who I think it is?" Olivia asked, doing her best to infuse her voice with a child-like excitement. The woman spun her head to look at the portrait Olivia had gestured to, letting out a small laugh.

"Oh, probably," she replied with a cryptic smile.

"Margaret's a stunt double," Lydia chimed in, giving her sister an adoring smile. "She's worked with loads of celebrities over the years."

Olivia almost choked on her tea. A stunt double was

the last occupation she would have assumed for the slight woman stood in front of her.

Her throat suddenly felt much too dry. *I guess that would explain the bruises and possibly the strength needed to throw a man over a balcony.*

"That's lovely," she forced, hoping her smile wasn't too wide. "It must be exciting to work on movie sets."

"It's a good way to pass the time," Margaret shrugged in agreement.

Silence lurked around the corner, threatening to expose Olivia's increased nervousness.

"Forgive me, I've had too much to drink already today. Would you mind if I use the loo?" she asked, clearing her throat.

Margaret looked a bit surprised, but her face quickly melted into the perfect 'hostess with the mostest' once again.

"Why, of course. It's just down the hall on your left," she offered, gesturing in the direction of the bathroom. "The lock sticks a little, but you won't get trapped in, don't worry."

Olivia quickly excused herself, doing her best to ignore the pounding of her pulse in her ears. She wanted to give Lawrence a glance but didn't trust herself to do so without giving away her suspicion that Margaret had moved up her suspects list.

The woman being a stunt double meant that she had to have some kind of strength. But enough to overpower a man like Simon and beat him to death?

It could just be coincidence, she reminded herself. *No need to be hasty.*

Still, Margaret's words echoed in her head. *Do you have a sister, detective?*

Olivia made a point of shutting the door to the bathroom, the loud thud of it pulling closed hopefully loud enough to signal that she was in fact using the toilet.

Instead, she started prodding around the room. She knew it wouldn't be admissible in a case, but she needed to know for herself before she began making accusations.

A quick search confirmed that Lydia's prescription sleeping pills were behind the mirror, along with various toiletries. *Lydia couldn't drive. Probably wouldn't have woken up if Margaret had done anything.* Dread started to build in Olivia's stomach with a certainty that made her know it was time to trust her instincts.

She poked around the bathroom for a few more moments but couldn't find anything else of note, try as she might. Anxiety clawed at her throat; she never much liked being in the house of a killer.

Flushing the toilet in attempt to mask her quick rummage, Olivia let the water run in the sink long enough to give herself a good long look in the mirror. Her auburn hair framed her face nicely, although her eyes clearly had a desperation to them that she hadn't had five minutes ago. *Calm down,* she urged herself. *Acting nervous isn't going to help anyone.* With a determination she wasn't sure came from confidence or masking her nerves, Olivia turned the tap off.

Loudly opening the door, she took precious seconds to scan the hallway. Photos of Margaret with various celebrities and on various set locations hung on the wall. None of which were incriminating.

Despite her rather physical job, everything else about her seemed tame. She liked drinking tea from fancy tea sets and, although seemingly single, she was happy, polite, welcoming, and friendly.

If she walked into the office with that list of traits, Collins would think she was a joke. A sweet woman with an interesting job? How did that suddenly make her a killer?

Fuck.

Olivia was now presented with a difficult decision: face Margaret head on or find more information first. Her pulse quickened once again as she weighed her options.

"...updates on the investigation," Lawrence's voice drifted into her awareness as she walked down the hall. She stood in the doorway of the lounge, unable to bring herself fully into the room. Both sisters looked up at her, as well as her partner.

"Is everything okay, detective?" Lydia asked, concern clearly written on her face. Lawrence looked even more befuddled.

Olivia took deep a breath and her eyes met with Margaret's, but before she could say another word, the sound of a phone ringing cut through the mounting tension.

Hers.

Bad timing, but the number was from DC Harris.

"Hi, it's Liv," she answered, turning away from the room. "Can I..."

Tim didn't give her a chance to finish her sentence.

"Francesca's walked in with some information," he blurted out. "I think it's important."

"Francesca?" Olivia echoed. *Shit. Super bad timing.* She almost had her claws into Margaret, though perhaps it was a blessing in disguise. If she barged into an altercation with the widow's sister on false accusations, it would be her own neck on the line. "Tell her I'm on my way," she hissed into the phone. "Make her comfortable, and don't let her leave until I get there."

She heard mumbling from the lounge; they'd clearly heard she was making an exit.

"Roger that!" Tim confirmed. "See you in a bit."

Olivia hung up and made her way back to where Lawrence was standing. He raised his eyebrows at her entrance, hoping for an update.

"We're needed back at the station," she breathed. Her eyes locked with Margaret's again, and the woman gave her an unreadable, confused expression.

"Nothing we've said, surely?" she asked wiping her palms on her dress. *Anxious?*

Olivia shook her head.

"No, not at all," she answered. "Just some new information has come up..." She looked over to Lawrence, her eyes telling him to step forward.

He excused himself from the midst of the women with a brief nod.

"Thank you, ladies," Liv offered once her partner was over the lounge threshold. He eased past her. "We'll be in touch, and we'll see ourselves out."

Both Lydia and Margaret looked confused as the detectives left, and Olivia trailed her partner outside and into the open. It was as if emerging from underwater after being there so long that she barely remembered how the outside world operated. Life exploded around her: moving cars and vibrant trees.

The spell of Margaret Anderson's household was broken.

22

"This had better be good," Lawrence mumbled as they parked at Newquay Police station. All she'd managed to tell him on the journey over, before she'd been caught up in a phone conversation with Clara, was that Margaret had suspicious bruising on her arm and somehow, her instinct told her the woman was involved in some way, shape or form.

"I agree," Olivia replied. "Perhaps we should tell Collins about what we think before we see Francesca?"

Lawrence laughed.

"What *you* think," he reiterated. "Besides, I'm not convinced, and there's just not enough evidence. You've seen how tiny the woman is. Stunt woman or not, can you honestly picture her overpowering our not-so-small Mr. Fisher, enough to batter the bugger to near death *and* throw him off the balcony? We need something concrete. Evidence that she's been lying or *something*. You know what CPS are like!"

Olivia nodded, slightly disappointed that her theory was being crumbled apart so easily, but she agreed with him. There would have been some kind of struggle, and a bruise on the wrist would have been the least of her worries.

They entered the station through the side door and were greeted by an awkwardly pacing DC Harris.

"Through here," he ushered them, relieved that he didn't have wait any longer. "We've got an appropriate adult with her. Not a parent or teacher. She wanted it that way." He added that part with a pointed look and lead them into one of their 'informal chat' rooms.

Francesca was sitting on a barely comfortable sofa alongside a woman with wild frizzy hair and a sympathetic expression on her face.

She stood when Olivia and Lawrence entered.

"Detectives," she greeted them.

Liv hadn't met her before, but Lawrence had.

"Cilla," he nodded. "This is my new partner, DI Austin."

"Pleased to meet you," Cilla smiled, turning to Liv. "Sorry it's under such unfortunate circumstances."

She gestured to the seats opposite and the detectives lowered themselves onto it.

Francesca was sitting with her hands in her lap, clasping them together.

They watched her intently, allowing her the time to

absorb the fact that it was a safe environment for her to air her worries in.

It was a moment before she spoke.

"I've found it hard," she croaked eventually. She gave a glance up to her AA who nodded encouragingly. Urging her to continue. "I miss him. I just... I'm..."

Olivia nodded gently. *In time you'll come to despise the man,* she thought to herself, but all the girl in front of her needed was to be reassured and soothed into speaking.

"You can do it," she offered with a light smile. "What made you come into the station today?"

Francesca looked up at one of the cameras and pulled at the sleeves on her jumper.

"Simon tried to leave me," she said quickly, almost wincing as though the acid words burnt her tongue on exit. "He said we'd been *caught,* and he had to leave me for a while..."

Olivia glanced at Lawrence briefly.

"Caught by who?" she urged. "His wife, *Mrs.* Fisher?"

Francesca shook her head.

"It was before she knew," the teen answered. "Before he had to admit everything. We were being watched by... by..." She stopped and swallowed then pushed her hair back from her face.

"Are you scared to tell us?" Lawrence asked gently. "No one can hurt you. We'll make sure of that."

Cilla nodded in agreement.

"Tell them," she whispered. "Tell them what you told me."

Francesca sighed. The angry fifteen-year-old girl from before had mostly gone now. Her eyes were red rimmed, and she sniffed and shrugged.

"We were being watched by his wife's sister," she said in a small voice. "She'd been following us, and she'd send him messages."—

Olivia crossed her legs to stop herself from jumping up and Lawrence leant forward.

"You mean, *she knew?*" Her partner asked. "We were under the assumption that she didn't and *still* doesn't know about your relationship. And you're sure it was her?"

Francesca nodded.

"A hundred percent," she confirmed. "We saw her car and watched her drive off. Her face and everything. Then he got the prank calls. No speaking, just calls. Simon said he couldn't handle it. Couldn't handle the risk of her saying something about who I was. He'd lose his job."

Olivia bit her bottom lip. This would aid her case tremendously when she presented evidence to Collins and the CPS about Margaret.

The woman had lied. She knew exactly why Lydia and Simon had split up. She knew and she'd seen it first-hand.

"Why didn't she tell Lydia?" Lawrence asked. "She didn't mention it to Mrs Fisher."

The teen reached forward and took a sip from her cup of water on the table that separated them.

"Not at the beginning," she answered. "But Simon went to speak to Mrs Fisher's sister. They met up, and that's when the death threats started, and he told me we had to stop. Things were getting bad. He told his wife everything. He confessed it all to her, so she heard it from him, and then I guess the next day he was killed."

Hold on.

Alarm bells rang in Olivia's head.

She was almost certain that she remembered Lydia telling them she forced the information out of a drunken Simon and that it had happened weeks before he'd been murdered.

Had the sisters been spinning a lie this whole time? Perhaps they were both in on the act. Maybe they worked in tandem to...

The knock at the door stopped her in her thoughts.

Bad timing yet again.

Francesca closed her mouth quickly, and Olivia almost saw all of her walls build up instantly.

DC Harris poked his head into the room without waiting to be called.

"Everything okay...?" Lawrence started, the hint of irritation laced his words. He too felt on the cusp of something.

Tim cleared his throat.

"There's been an incident!" he said quickly. "An

ongoing incident. Can I...?" He gestured to them to step out of the room.

Olivia stood up, followed by Dean.

"Excuse us for a moment," she apologised to Francesca before they left. "You've done so well, already."

Outside in the hall, Lawrence pressed his hands into his pockets and raised his brows. The winter sun burned the imprint of the window onto the wall beside him.

"What's this about?" he asked.

DC Harris looked at his notepad.

"Um, dispatch had a concern for welfare call come through," he answered quickly. "It was called in by a *Lydia Fisher*. Your widow."

"*Fuck!*" Lawrence growled. "Who is it for?"

"Margaret," Tim sighed. "Officers and paramedics have been dispatched, but apparently she's asked for... you." He turned to Olivia.

"Me?" she asked incredulously. He nodded. "Damnit. You don't think this is due to our visit, do you?"

Lawrence jangled the keys in his pocket.

"Who cares," he replied. "We need to get down there *now*. Harris, give our apologies to Francesca. We'll get her statement later."

"On it." He tore out a page of his notepad. "Here's the info. All we know is she left the house and could be heading for the cliffs at Huers Hut. We're waiting for more information, though. I'll text you en route."

That was all they needed to hear.

The duo left the station and ran to their car. Olivia could feel the adrenalin coursing through her veins as they weaved amongst the traffic.

"Maybe she would rather die with her secret than confess?" Lawrence assumed. "Any more details, yet? We can go to Huers Hut, and if she's not there, circle back along the coast until we hear something?"

Olivia's phone pinged, and she found a message from Tim.

"Tolcarne Beach confirmed," she read. "Officers and HART in attendance. Cliff side of the fence. Shit, she's really thinking of jumping, Dean!"

Lawrence, pulled the car over, turned around and put his foot down. The beach wasn't far from the police station, but with the constant stream of tourists whenever the sun shone, it took them longer than usual to drive the short distance.

Once there, they pulled up and parked amidst a sea of commotion. Bystanders hovered, eagerly awaiting any kind of drama that presented itself, and Olivia got a sudden sense of dread.

"Police, coming through!" she called over the crowd until she reached the cordon.

To her surprise, PC Andrew Shaw was stood here, all formal looking in his uniform. He saw her but kept his professional posture apart from a brief wink.

She could almost feel the smirk on her back from

Lawrence as they ducked under the tape, her heels instantly sinking slightly into the mud.

Up ahead, she could see Lydia being comforted by an officer, and further on, Margaret stood, her back to everyone, clad in the same clothes she'd been wearing earlier, but this time coupled with a billowing blonde wig. *Possibly the hair found in Fisher's wound?*

A paramedic incident commander appeared at their side.

"Detective Inspector Olivia Austin?" he asked, his face grave. She nodded. "Over here."

She followed him along the grass until they reached Lydia.

"What happened?" she asked. "How did it go from Darjeeling *to this?*"

Mrs. Fisher seemed distressed, her face pink and swollen from worry and crying.

"When you left, she couldn't settle," Lydia answered. "Pacing the room. Wondering what you were called away for... I've never seen her like that before."

Because she's guilty, that's why. Olivia thought to herself. Margaret must have panicked when the call came through. She probably thought it was evidence against her, that she was about to be pounced upon.

"Liv." It was Lawrence's voice, urging her to wrap it up and see to the woman at hand. After all, that was the reason they were there, and they'd both agreed in the car not to mention Simon or their suspicions that she was the one who'd killed him.

She approached the fence slowly with the paramedic incident commander.

"Margaret, it's DI Austin," she offered smoothly. "But you can call me Liv."

There was silence for a moment, and the terrified woman didn't at first acknowledge that she was being spoken to.

"Margar—"

"I know you're there," she interjected, her icy tone settling on Olivia's ears. It was no match, however, for the coldness she already felt despite the sun.

"Then come over and let's talk about this," she offered. "You wanted to speak to me. Am I correct?"

Margaret looked over her shoulder briefly.

"I don't want to put Lydia through any more of this craziness," she answered wearily. "She's been through enough already! We both have!"

The incident commander gave her a nod to keep going. She hadn't been trained as a negotiator but being called for by name meant something at least.

"What else do you think she'd go through if you jumped?" Olivia asked. "She's distraught. She needs you. You don't want to cause her any more pain, do you?"

Margaret shook her head. The comment struck her deeper than intended because it caused her to almost launch herself off the cliff. There was mini outcry of panic as everyone braced themselves.

"Stop! Wait, stop!" Olivia called out. *Always saying the*

wrong things, she thought to herself. She could feel Lawrence watching her closely, seeing what she would say and do next, and he had every reason to be concerned. This next question was going to go deep and against everything they'd discussed in their mini briefing on the way over, but it had to be said. She had to touch on her suspicions.

The slight wind whipped around them, and the voices of bystanders stilled into the distance.

"Is all of this because of Simon?" Olivia's words hung in the air despite the weight of them. "Because he's dead, or because you *killed* him?"

At the sound of his name, Margaret's body tensed, and slowly she stepped back, much to Olivia's relief and surprise.

"Don't say his name," she called over her shoulder, her voice still just as dead as before. "He doesn't deserve to be remembered. Not anymore. Not to me!"

Lydia appeared at Liv's side, the coat in her hands held up to cover her quivering mouth.

The incident commander put a hand on Olivia's elbow and leaned into her.

"I've been informed by the Coastguard that wind speed is picking up," he whispered into her ear.

She hummed her acknowledgement and glanced over at Lawrence. He looked concerned, rubbing at his chin in deep contemplation.

There was one part of her theory that she hadn't gone over with him. In fact, the idea had seemed so incomprehensible at first that she hadn't allowed herself to explore the magnitude of her thoughts.

She cleared her throat, aware that a crying Lydia was still by her side. It would be a shock to her too.

"You loved him, Margaret, didn't you?" Olivia asked against the strengthening wind. It was clear now. The whole rigmarole of being the overprotective sister, the façade of anger that she forced everyone around her to believe. She cared more than she let on. And this? This show on top of a cliff had passion written all over it.

Beside her, she heard Lydia's sharp intake of breath at the enormity of the revelation.

Margaret covered her face in her hands and shook her head.

"It's not true, *is it?*" Lydia asked, her voice wavering ever so slightly and was that a hint of anger she detected in it? "Tell me it's not true!"

It was that question that caused Margaret to look back over her shoulder fully for the first time. Her eyes locked with Olivia's, full of desperation and anguish.

"How would I have ever told you?" she snapped, this addressed to her sister. "It was before you met him. Before you knew he existed!"

Lydia wailed loudly.

"I married him!" she shouted. "You could have told me then! Stopped me from making the biggest mistake of my life!"

Olivia stepped back slightly to allow the sisters space to express themselves.

"I saw how happy you were with him," Margaret responded, her voice more hurt than defensive of her actions. "Despite how I felt about him, he made you smile again."

Lydia walked right up to the fence and pressed her body against it.

"I could have been happy with somebody else." She sighed and hung her head. "That wasn't your choice to make."

Her sister poised herself for jumping again, and two uniformed officers lifted themselves over the fence to make their way toward her, as did some of the Hazardous Area Response Team. She was crying now, more so than before, and the Incident Commander pulled Lydia back. She'd done enough.

Keep her talking though. Olivia thought deciding to take over and bring her line of question onto the murder. She was almost certain now that the woman standing in front of her looking down the side of the cliff face was responsible for the death of Simon Fisher.

"Why did you do it?" She pushed her voice to carry over the sound of the waves below them. "Were you genuinely angry at what he did? At his affair? For hurting your sister? Or was it jealousy?"

Margaret shook her head vigorously.

"I despised him in the end," she spat. "For what he did to me *and* my sister. The betrayal of our love." she paused, turning to look at one of the officers approaching her. "For what he did to that young girl."

Lawrence stepped forward, unable to resist.

"Then why didn't you call the police?" he asked. "Why not report him? Why take matters into your own hands and risk all of this?" He gestured around them to the scene that had been created—at the throng of spectators that had gathered on top and below the cliff to witness her fall to her death.

She was silent for a moment, looking out to the cloudless sky with the hem of her dress flapping in the wind. The blonde wig she had on was dishevelled and sliding to one side slightly. Despite all her misgivings, she looked like a small, weary child at the end of a meltdown.

She turned toward Olivia and slowly walked back up to the fence. Her eyes were swollen from crying.

"I... I saw red," she whispered. "I saw my sister broken at my door, and it took me back..."

"Margie no!" Lydia hissed, but the woman wouldn't be silenced.

She shook her head.

"Our dad used to.... he used to, with Lyds, he would..." She could barely form the words, but Olivia knew what she was trying to say. The sick, fucking bastard.

"It's okay," she soothed.

"But it's not okay, is it?" Margaret sobbed. "I followed him and his student to a carpark, and what I watched him do... What he did to her... I saw red and then, well... I wasn't supposed to kill him. I just wanted to teach him a lesson. You know that men like him are sick. It went too far. He knew I saw him. He knew that I knew, and when I was beating him, I just saw my dad. I saw that evil man creeping into Lyds' room. The things he did to her... and I just couldn't stop. Simon betrayed both of our trust. He..." She broke down into body shaking sobs.

Lawrence groaned beside her, his hate for any domestic violence or abuse against women brimming to the surface.

Olivia reached out and put her hand on Margaret's, squeezing it to reassure the woman that she understood her hurt and the delicate nature of the information she had provided.

"There's help available for the both of you," she soothed. "You don't have to suffer through years of grief alone. Left raw, this is what it can turn into."

Take heed, Liv, she told herself.

Lawrence, however, watched the woman crying, his brow furrowed, and once a few moments had passed, he turned to the widowed sister.

"What was your role in your husband's murder?" he asked, their tale of woe not quite pacifying him.

"I had no part in any of it!" Lydia assured firmly. She seemed surprised at being addressed. "I hated him, yes, but he was still my husband, Detective. My job means I help keep people alive, not *kill* them!"

"Then why lie to us?" Olivia added, remembering Francesca's words. "You told us Simon drunkenly confirmed the affair?"

She nodded, defeat weighing her shoulders down.

"I was in shock," she breathed. "And I knew how it would and *did* look. My husband was sleeping with a young teenager, and then the day after he confesses and I ask him for a divorce, he's found dead. You would have pinned it on me. I've seen what happens when the police believe you're guilty."

The detectives exchanged pointed looks.

"That still doesn't explain the murder," Lawrence noted. This time, he turned to Margaret, who had managed to ease her sobs. Her head was hung low, and for the last part of the conversation, she'd been starting at the grass that framed the fence. "If you were alone, how did you manage to throw Simon over the balcony? How did you overpower a man as *big* as he was with barely any injury?" He gestured to her bruised wrist.

The woman looked up for the first time in minutes, her eyes finding each of theirs in turn.

"Adrenalin," she answered, her voice no higher than a whisper. Olivia squinted against the wind to hear her better. "When he first saw me, he fell, and I seized the opportunity to get him while he was down." She swallowed back more tears. "I panicked when I realised how far I'd gone, and I wanted it to look like suicide. Then I threw up in the toilet twice at the sight of all the blood. I just... I can't... I'm so sorry!"

Lydia reached across the fence to pull her sister in toward her, wrapping her arms around her shoulders as they cried together, all feelings of hate and anger evaporating with each passing second.

The officers reached her side before she had a chance to move away, and along with HART they had her safe and secured.

For now, her ordeal was over.

23

The rest of the afternoon passed by in a blur, between getting Margaret to the custody suite for booking and having her mentally assessed.

Olivia and Lawrence had agreed that there was a good chance Margaret could and would plead temporary insanity in her case, and that they'd support the decision by her legal team if she did.

Olivia had also texted Mills partway through the day. *Just wanted to say I love you. We should get a bite to eat soon.*

I'd love that. Tough case? her sister had replied moments later.

I'll tell you over lunch tomorrow, Olivia had shot back, quiet gratitude thrumming in her chest.

"This one's been difficult," Lawrence admitted quietly as they started on the mountain of paperwork back at the office.

Liv let out a long, slow breath and reclined her swivel chair a little. Her stomach grumbled, and she realised that in all the haste of the day, she'd forgotten to eat.

"You can say that again," she agreed. A phone rang somewhere out in the main office, and the sound of laughter drifted in through the open window. She closed her eyes against the ceiling lights to allow herself a moment.

She couldn't even begin to imagine the horror that those two women had to deal with growing up. The fear and pain of carrying that burden all these years didn't bear thinking about, but the way Simon Fisher had been murdered and the injuries he'd suffered made her shudder. There were so many layers to the case that she knew the next couple of days would be hectic, to say the least.

Her silent reflection was broken by a knock at their office door, and Detective Superintendent Collins entered and stopped with his arm resting against the frame.

"You did an excellent job, guys." He nodded once he had both of their attention. "Some officers on scene said you kept your heads throughout."

"Thank you, sir," Olivia smiled. "There were a few moments where I thought she'd jump, but her background was..."

"Horrific," he finished for her. Someone came up

behind and tapped him on the shoulder. He spoke to them briefly before turning back to the detectives. "Epson went out and brought some snacky type things for the office." He waved his fingers dismissively. "Have a quick break and a bite. All in the kitchen for you."

He hovered in the doorway for a moment longer, his expression one of gratitude, until he nodded and excused himself.

"Well, can't think of a better timing," Lawrence said, the first to speak once their boss had disappeared back to his office. "I'm absolutely *Hank Marvin*! I know you are too! I've heard your stomach going ten to the dozen for the last fifteen minutes!"

Olivia stretched and stood up.

"Is it greedy of me to hope there's an apple turnover with my name on it?" she asked, already at the door.

Lawrence laughed and made his way over to her.

"That's wishful thinking," he observed. "It was Epson after all. You're probably looking at a multi-pack of doughnuts from Aldi across the road. *Jam* if we're lucky!"

Olivia couldn't help the grin that spread across her face at her partner's words, and before they left the safe confines of their office, she put her arm out to hold him back.

"We're okay, though, aren't we?" she asked, offering him a hopeful smile that after their little fall out earlier they'd be able to go back to how things were before she let her anger and hurt get the better of her.

Lawrence squeezed her shoulder in agreement, returning her grin.

"*More* than okay," he assured her. "Now, let's get you fed!"

"You did *not!*" Clara gasped laughing, halfway into her second cocktail of the evening. Olivia swirled her own drink, glancing down at it with a smirk sprawled across her lips.

"Let's just say, he stopped messing with me after that," Olivia replied before tossing back a solid swig.

"Olivia!" Clara exclaimed, her eyes wide. "I never knew I needed stories from your uni days so desperately until tonight!"

The two had been at the bar for a couple of hours, swapping stories back and forth. To Olivia's relief, neither of them even touched the comings and goings of work. It felt good to talk about something other than casefiles and work drama, and Olivia knew that the warmth kissing her cheeks was from more than just the alcohol. Clara's company was easy and delightful.

"I can't even imagine what kind of shenanigans you got up to in your youth. Oh wait, you still *are* in your youth," Olivia shot back with a hearty laugh.

Clara nudged her jokingly.

"What can I say? Young, beautiful, and brilliant!" Her teeth flashed as she spoke, all dazzle and spectacle.

There was no denying that the two women were quite different. Clara was all about performance, while Olivia tended to try and observe from the shadows.

Maybe that was what made them click so well.

"I have to ask," Olivia murmured, suddenly aware that she might be tipsier than she initially thought. "Are you and Hershel still...*you know?*"

Clara smiled knowingly.

"We may or may not be going on a date tomorrow," she practically whispered, ducking her head to explain to Olivia, who widened her eyes at the comment.

"That's lovely!" she exclaimed, giving her friend's hand an eager squeeze. "You'll have to let me know how it goes!"

Clara shrugged before slyly taking a sip of her Gimlet.

"Who knows if it'll go anywhere," she admitted. "But I actually quite like her."

Olivia thought that for maybe the first time, Clara was actually trying to *hide* a smile.

"I'm happy for you," she hummed, mulling over her wine.

"And you?" The tech analyst asked. "Are you going to hit up Duracell again?" Olivia nearly spat her wine out at Clara's question. "Sorry—forgot that was a sore subject."

"First of all, I never *hit up* Constable Shaw," she defended unable to hold back the tipsy grin on her face at the comment. "Believe me, I've thought about it, but I don't know if it'd be a good idea. Besides..." Olivia sighed, holding back for a moment, trying to gauge whether or not she was ready to talk about the more serious things with Clara. *She makes me feel safe*, she realised as she glanced up at the tech analyst, who was avidly studying her facial expressions as she sipped her cocktail. "I'm not sure that I'm quite ready to take on a real relationship right now," she admitted, looking down at her hands.

There was a moment of silence between them before she felt Clara squeeze her shoulder, and she gave her a grateful look in return.

"Maybe I am," she added. "I just don't want to rush things."

"Take as much time as you need," Clara insisted. "That being said, it doesn't always have to lead to a relationship. You could always just...wham bam, thank you ma'am and onto the next!"

"Clara!" Olivia felt her cheeks flush with more than just the wine but found herself laughing.

"I'm just saying!" She giggled as she spoke, putting Olivia at ease. "If you want to roll around with Duracell in his bed, fuck what the office has to say about it. We women enjoy sex just as much as men."

She shrugged.

"Maybe you're right," Liv acquiesced with a small smile. "Maybe he's just what I need right now."

Clara nodded slowly.

"Exactly," she replied, tone surprisingly soft. "You just do you, babe. Don't worry about anyone else."

Olivia knew the tech analyst was right. Perhaps the assumption that every man she met might be a replacement for Rhys was holding her back. Having fun whilst healing wasn't something to be ashamed of.

"I'll try my best," she acknowledged.

The two talked well into the night, swapping stories and discussing their lives. Warmth bloomed in Olivia; they seemed to get each other so well.

It'd been a while since she'd had a true woman friend —besides her sister, of course. It was hard in a men-dominated field to find lasting friendships—not to mention her reservations about strong ties on the force since the incident last year, and many of the ones she had made disappeared as the months went on, their own awkwardness at not knowing what to say preventing them from saying anything.

Clara was different. She had an uncanny way of encouraging Olivia to bring her walls down.

As they exchanged their goodbyes, Olivia felt bolstered up, as if she were a wilting plant that finally had been watered.

"We'll grab another drink soon, yeah?" Clara asked, preparing to climb out of their joint Uber.

"Of course," Olivia agreed, a wide grin on her face. "To new friendships!" She beamed, raising an imaginary glass.

"To new friendships!" Clara called back.

Olivia smiled her whole way home, almost waltzing around the cottage as she got ready for bed. The words played over and over in her mind like an ode to the next morning's sunrise. *To new friendships.*

The End - (*Go to Book Three, Kiss and Hell*)

Can't wait for Book Three? Here it is!
http://getbook.at/KissAndHell

Missed Book One? Don't worry, it's here!
http://getbook.at/FindTheGirl

LOVE TO READ DETECTIVE THRILLERS?

Join my Newsletter to be the first to hear about New Releases and ARC opportunities.

http://eepurl.com/hskzML

ABOUT THE AUTHOR

I've always had a passion for writing stories and loved being able to create a world and have my characters live inside it. Being able to do this has been a dream come true and I'm so grateful that you could join me on this journey .
I live in the United Kingdom with my Husband and four young children who keep me busy and who I wouldn't ever be without.
I hope you enjoy reading my books and please feel free to join me on social media where I love to interact with my readers!

mrsrobertswrites@hotmail.com

facebook.com/mrsrobertswrites

Printed in Great Britain
by Amazon